D0976022

HAUNTED WATERS

HAUNTED WATERS

MARY POPE OSBORNE

CANDLEWICK PRESS
CAMBRIDGE, MASSACHUSETTS

Copyright © 1994, 2006 by Mary Pope Osborne

Revised edition 2006

Library of Congress Cataloging-in-Publication Data

Osborne, Mary Pope.
Haunted waters / Mary Pope Osborne. —Rev. ed.
p. cm.
Summary: After meeting the mysterious sea maid Undine on a bleak promontory and making her his wife, Lord Huldbrand tries to defend her from the faceless demon that haunts her, while he probes her strange ties to the aquatic world.
ISBN-13: 978-0-7636-2995-3
ISBN-10: 0-7636-2995-2
[1. Supernatural—Fiction. 2. Water—Fiction. 3. Fantasy.]
I. La Motte-Fouqué, Friedrich Heinrich Karl, Freiherr de, 1777–1843.
Undine. English. II. Title.
PZ7.O81167Hau   2006
[Fic]—dc22   2005058160

2 4 6 8 10 9 7 5 3 1

Printed in the United States of America

This book was typeset in Centaur.

Candlewick Press
2067 Massachusetts Avenue
Cambridge, Massachusetts 02140

visit us at www.candlewick.com

For Natalie

Dear Reader,

Like many authors, I rarely go back and read a book I've written once it's been published. But when Candlewick Press announced it was planning to reissue my novel *Haunted Waters,* I felt compelled to glance at the text again.

Haunted Waters was originally published twelve years ago, and an odd thing happened when I re-entered the dark forest on the back of Sir Huldbrand's horse. By the time we had found our way to the hut of the beautiful sea spirit, Undine, waves crashed again on the shore, fresh fires crackled in the hearth, and characters I hadn't visited in years sprang to life. Huldbrand and Undine's story was basically the same, but I began to feel they wanted it told in a slightly different way. Had they changed? Had I? Or had all of us grown a bit since we last loved and suffered together?

My editor at Candlewick, Amy Ehrlich, was generous, open-minded, and even pleased when I presented her with a revised manuscript of the knight and sea spirit's tale. And this is the scary truth I've learned: stories are living things, and we who write them must beware of entering their forests a second time.

Mary Pope Osborne

One

A decaying odor filled the air. Eyes seemed to be watching me: eyes as cold and wet as the slime that covered the tree trunks all around me. I felt weak with dread as my horse trod beneath a canopy of still, skeletal branches, deeper and deeper into the dark woods.

Only a short while before, traveling from my estate at Ringstetten to the duke's castle in St. Martin, I'd come upon a path between the ancient trees. Wondering if perhaps it had been cleared by the duke's gamesmen, I gave way to the spirit of adventure and began to follow it.

Soon, however, I became lost. The forest closed around me. I desperately wished to return to the well-traveled road, but with each step of my horse, the gnarled undergrowth seemed to close over my exit. Now the woods were so damp that water dripped from the tree arms crooking above me. Though not a bird's cry nor a squirrel's skitter helped to liven the thick, dungeonlike air, I felt as if I were not alone.

Suddenly the air grew colder. The wind started to blow. Branches clattered like dry bones. High-pitched laughter rippled through the forest, then grew louder and louder. My horse's ears went back.

Ahead of us, out of the shadows, a demon appeared. Shrouded in a diaphanous cloak, its face was not human—no lips, no eyes—only black holes in a white mask of skin.

I screamed, and the demon sailed away through the windy, howling woods. I pulled on my reins, but my horse galloped forward, crashing through the undergrowth.

Screeching with laughter, the specter glided ahead of us, threading its way through the trees as if it were made of vapor.

With all my might, I reined in my horse, pulled him to a halt, and forced him around. But as we bolted away, we were suddenly plunged into a raging water-fall. The cascade sent me headlong to the ground. Fearing I would surely drown, I dragged myself from beneath the battering torrent and collapsed upon the earth.

Lying in the mud, I heard the wind subside and the hideous laughter cease. The waterfall dwindled to almost nothing—a thin trickle down the side of a glistening black boulder.

The demon was gone. He had lured me deep into the woods, then vanished.

Still the forest breathed evil. What other spirits haunted its shadows? Ghouls who gnawed the bones of the dead? Wolf men who ate the living? Vampires who sucked their blood?

As I lay soaked and battered, sprawled in the rotting marsh, a soft singing wafted through the gloom: a voice, cracked and whispery, singing the Psalms.

I dragged myself from the ground and limped to

my horse. I pulled myself onto his back, and we began to move cautiously toward the song. Brighter and brighter sunlight penetrated the brush. Eventually, my horse carried me out of the woods onto a seacoast ablaze with sunset.

A small hillock rose from the marshy edge of the forest and jutted into the ocean. Chickens roamed the sparse peninsula, and a simple hut made of mud and thatch rested on the slope. A fisherman sat in the doorway, mending his nets. As he sang his song of praise, long, lean cats lounged near his feet.

My horse neighed and began to move toward the hut. The cats dashed away and the fisherman froze at the sight of us.

I tried to imagine what he saw: the tattered knight's raiment hanging from my limbs—the soaked mantle and torn tunic—and the drenched plume of red feathers dangling from my cap.

I dismounted and stepped toward the peasant. "Good evening, friend," I said hoarsely. "I am Lord Huldbrand of Ringstetten. I am traveling to St. Martin to see the duke."

Open-mouthed, he stared at me as if I were an apparition.

"I was thrown from my horse when he charged into a waterfall," I said.

I held his gaze for another moment. Then he grinned, his face breaking into rivulets of wrinkles. He dropped his nets and moved quickly to soothe my skittish horse. Then he looked at me. "You must rest here, my lord," he said kindly.

I sighed with relief. "Thank you, friend. I need shelter for only one night. Then I must be on my way to St. Martin."

From the distance came a sudden ripple of laughter. My eyes darted to the shadowed forest. A white shape seemed to lurk beneath a swaying willow. My horse whinnied in fright.

"Praise God!" said the fisherman.

The specter vanished.

"What is it?" I whispered. "What monster lives there?"

The fisherman shook his shoulders as if shaking free from the unearthly sight. "Many things are seen and heard in the dark woods, my lord. Come, let us go in." And he lifted the wooden latch of his door and led the way inside.

A hearth fire glowed in the single room of the hut.

The floor was made of pounded earth covered with dried rushes. A hen sat in a box of straw near the fireplace, and an enormous pile of sheepskins billowed along the back wall.

"Lord Huldbrand of Ringstetten," the fisherman said to someone in the corner.

I turned and looked upon a frail, stooped woman clutching her sewing to her chest.

Removing my wet cap, I bowed. "Forgive me, madam, but I need shelter for the night."

The woman whimpered and looked at her husband.

"Where is Undine?" he gently asked her.

She gestured with a trembling hand.

"Our child is by the sea," he explained.

I was startled; I could not imagine this elderly couple had a child.

The fisherman went to the door and called,

"Undine!" Then he helped remove my wet mantle and bade me sit near the fire.

Watching him stir a black cauldron, I inhaled the scent of wood smoke and a fishy-smelling broth, and my heart felt strangely peaceful. This simple, crude dwelling seemed as serene and good as the woods had seemed evil.

The door flew open and, not a child, but a young woman stood on the threshold. Her hair was drenched with seawater and her face was rose-tinted by the late afternoon light. She stared at me with a gaze as innocent and open as a fawn's.

"My lord, this is our daughter, Undine," said the fisherman.

Two

Undine was as still as a statue.

"Lord Huldbrand of Ringstetten was on his way to St. Martin," the fisherman told her, "but he became lost in our woods."

Undine slowly moved toward me and touched the gold medallion that hung from a chain around my neck. "How lovely," she said in a clear, silvery voice.

She held my gaze with her light blue eyes, the color of the sunlit sea. Her dark, wet hair rippled down over a blue smock.

"Undine," her father said in a scolding voice.

She paid no heed but let her eyes slowly wander over my face.

"Daughter, have modesty," the fisherman said.

She gave him a quick smile, then turned to the fire and began to stir the soup cauldron.

"Come, let us sit down to our supper," said the fisherman. He closed the door, shutting out the last light of day. As his wife watched from the corner, he poured wine into goblets and set a chunk of black bread on the heavy oaken table.

"Please share our supper, my lord," he said.

I joined them at the table, and the fisherman dipped three wooden bowls into the pot on the hearth. He gave one to me, one to himself, and one to Undine and her mother to share.

By flickering candlelight, I watched the two women take turns sipping their broth. Undine kept her gaze upon me even as she broke the hard bread and offered some to her feeble mother. I felt lightheaded in the glow of the fire. The fish soup, the dark wine, Undine's pale eyes—all held me in a sort of ecstatic embrace.

No one spoke until the bowls had been cleared. Then Undine said in a voice as soft as the wind, "Tell us, my lord, what do men do in the land where you live?"

Touched by her formal speech, I smiled. I imagined she had not spoken to many strangers in her life. "I am afraid we do a great deal that means nothing," I said.

"Yes?" she asked.

"Actually, my castle is quite busy in the summer," I said, hastening to answer her question without mockery. "There is hay making and . . ." I could barely remember the activity at my castle as her bewitching eyes stared intently at me.

"What else?" she said.

"Well, there is pulling the flax and shearing the wool from the sheep," I stammered.

"So you make hay and pull flax and shear sheep?" she asked.

"No. I—I supervise my workers."

"You sit on your horse and tell everyone what to do?"

"Daughter," her father reprimanded her.

But she persisted with a smile. "You tell everyone what to do, my lord? Is that right?"

"Well, I—I imagine that—" I was having difficulty answering her; her bold gaze and direct manner had frozen my tongue.

"You *imagine* that is what you do?" she said.

Suddenly the fisherman's wife screamed and pointed at the window. A white form swayed in the dark. I grabbed my sword and rushed to the door.

"Wait!" cried the fisherman.

I paid no heed and stepped out of the hut into the twilight.

There was no sign of the apparition. Only the trill of an owl and the croak of a frog came from the woods. Sea breezes whispered in the reeds, and wavelets rhythmically slapped the shore.

A bony hand clasped my arm, and I jumped. "Your sword will not protect you," said the fisherman. "Our weapons are useless against the supernatural."

"But what is this thing?" I said.

"A lost soul," he said in a low voice, "a godforsaken spirit. His presence has driven my poor wife mad."

A bird cried from the sea. Thunder rumbled in the distance. Fear filled my soul, for we seemed powerless, this old man and I, against the forces of the night.

Rain began to tap upon the leaves and ground.

"Shall we go in?" I said.

"Aye."

I followed the fisherman back into the hut, and he bolted the door against the dark. The fire in the hearth still burned fiercely, and shadows danced on the walls.

I wanted to see Undine again, to redeem my pride. But she had retired to the back of the hut with her mother. I heard her whispering comforting words to the frightened woman.

"Come, my lord, sleep here by our fire," the fisherman said.

He spread a sheepskin near the hearth, and I lay down on the primitive bed and soon drifted toward a dream. As snores came from the back of the room, I thought I heard someone move across the floor and the door open and the wind howl but, too weary even to lift my head, I fell into a deep slumber.

 Three

All night my sleep was as restless as the weather. In and out of dreams, I heard the wind and rain pummel the hut. I sensed Undine was awake, even close by. I imagined at one point that she was stroking my hair. I rose toward waking, but a dream of her pulled me back into the dark waters of sleep.

At dawn, cold air blew across my face. I opened my eyes and saw the door ajar. Daylight streamed in, along with a clean, biting wind.

I rose and stepped outside to find Undine with her father. They were staring silently at their land. The willows and oaks at the edge of the woods were broken and leaning as if they had been whipped by a tyrant.

The gentle stream that had flowed to the sea and meandered across one end of the peninsula had changed into a rushing torrent. The waters now severed the fisherman's land from the woods, transforming the peninsula into an island.

Undine looked at me, her pale blue eyes sparkling in the light. "I think you cannot leave today," she said. She smiled, then turned and walked down toward the shore.

Throughout the morning, the floodwaters raced around the bottom of the hill, delaying my departure. I felt less trapped by the wild stream, however, than by my fascination with Undine. As I sat on the sparse windy slope above the sea, my eyes never left her. I watched her help her father smoke his fish over a pit fire of seaweed and driftwood. Then she and her frail mother gathered wild plants by the stream.

Around midday, Undine carried a willow basket filled with laundry down to the sea. She waded into the stormy tide and dunked the blue-and-mustard-colored garments into the water.

After she had spread the clothes over rocks to dry, she raced toward the waves and dove beneath a churning surface of foam and uprooted weeds. Soon emerging, she shook out her hair, then rolled over one wave and another. For long periods, she vanished beneath the broken sea while storm petrels circled above the waves, frantically cawing, as if begging her to return.

I could not imagine how she swam so long beneath the surface. At one point, I thought she had disappeared forever, but then I saw her rise from the water, glistening with spray, her blue smock clinging to her long, graceful limbs.

In the afternoon, I whittled a bow while the fisherman and Undine worked together, seining the water for the day's catch. As they dragged their fish-filled nets through the shallow waves, I was lulled into a feeling of deep serenity.

But with the coming of dark, I felt the return of fear. The woods were alive with strange cries, the stars unnaturally close and bright. I sought sanctuary before the fisherman's hearth. With the door bolted and a cup of wine, I found comfort in the sight of Undine stirring the seafood broth and raking the coals of the fire.

In the middle of the night, I woke suddenly. The fisherman was snoring. The door opened, then closed. Someone moved across the earthen floor.

"Who goes there?" I asked, sitting up.

"Me," Undine whispered.

She seemed to be returning from the sea. When she came near, though I could barely see her by the dim light of the fire, I could almost feel the breath of the midnight ocean: its salty freshness and chill.

"You were swimming?" I said.

"Yes."

"You are not afraid to swim at night?"

"No, I love to swim in the dark, beneath the waves."

"Why?" I whispered.

"It brings me closer to the heart of the sea."

"The heart of the sea?"

"Yes."

"What is that?"

"It is hard to find," she said in a soft voice, "but sometimes if you are hidden by fog or the darkness of night, you can feel the ocean's heartbeat."

"Indeed?" I could not imagine what she meant. I assumed she spoke poetry.

"You can hear the music then, too," she said. "Fish sing. You know this?"

"No," I said, "I did not know this."

She sighed, then stood. "Well, they do," she whispered.

"What does their song sound like?" I said.

"Listen for it in your sleep," she said. Then she retreated to the back of the hut, into the shadows. And for the rest of the night, eerie, high-pitched singing threaded its way through my dreams.

Four

The roaring stream imprisoned me for days. Each morning I watched Undine dive beneath the silver waves. As she slid in and out of the sea, I imagined her to be a sea maid living in a time when the earth was very young and all life rose from the fathomless deep. Her strength and mystery made me remember the sirens who had bewitched ancient sailors, sending them to watery deaths.

One night before sleep, when I heard her slip out of the hut, I rose from my sheepskin and followed.

Outside, I saw her moving in the distance, down a path of moonlight to the shore.

I trailed after her through the cold night air, stepping cautiously, wary of haunting figures who might be lurking beyond our white path. As I drew closer to her, I heard a simple song. It was not sung in a language I knew. Devastatingly beautiful and sad, the song curled through the night and seemed to draw soft whispers back from the sea.

Then the singing stopped. In the moonlight, I saw Undine's silhouette: she was sitting on a rock, staring at me.

"I am sorry," I said. "I did not mean to startle you."

She was silent.

"Were you singing to the fish?"

She did not answer.

"Would you rather I go?"

"No," she said. "You may sit with me, Lord Huldbrand."

Feeling entirely under her command, I moved closer and sat on the edge of her rock.

"Tell me about your home," she said.

"My home is very different from yours," I said. "There is no sea. Only a river, a peaceful river."

"And you live on the river?"

"No. I live in a castle some distance away. It was my father's. It is made of stone and sits on top of a hill surrounded by walls. Below is a meadow with sheep. And I have vineyards. I sell my wine and wool at the market in St. Martin."

"I would like to visit your home someday," she said.

Pleased and surprised, I quickly said, "Oh, yes, perhaps you can."

"I like you, Lord Huldbrand," she said.

As the salty wind swept against me, I felt joyful. Gaining her approval and affection made me feel as if I had gained the good opinion of Nature herself.

"But——" she said, "you are not as wise as you might seem."

"No?"

"There are questions you have never asked, Lord Huldbrand. There are worlds you have never imagined."

I wondered if she was speaking of the phantom, of the dark woods and the sea. But before I could ask her, she stood and began moving across the sand.

"Wait—" I called.

But she splashed into the waves before I could go on. I hurried to the edge of the sea and stared after her. She had vanished beneath the rolling black waters. Nothing seemed more forlorn or ominous to me than the ocean at night. I was frightened by its relentless flow and its colossal indifference.

I could not follow her.

Neither could I wait for her, for I felt afraid and ashamed now in the cold, clammy dark. The wind blew hard as I retreated up the hill.

Five

I slept restlessly until dawn. Before I rose from my bed, I made the decision to follow Undine into the waves this day.

As soon as I stepped out of the hut into the early morning, I caught sight of her swimming in the distance. As if in a trance, I moved down the slope to the cool, gray shore. I pulled off my boots and tunic and dove into the crashing surf.

The undertow was greater than I had imagined. I struggled to stay above the waves. When I looked farther out to sea, I could not see her. Had she left the water?

I glanced back at the beach. Terror washed over me. The white form of the demon was wafting over the gray shore.

Then suddenly the specter vanished as if blown away by the wind, and in the next instant I was yanked beneath the waves.

I felt as if I were shackled by an iron current. Try as I might, I could not rise to the surface. I thrashed wildly against the water, until Undine grabbed my arm and pulled me up to the air through a splash of foam and spray. I could breathe again. The water was calmer, and for a moment, we seemed to dance together, bobbing in a pool of jeweled light.

Then Undine broke away and started to swim out to sea. I followed, and we swam together through serene blue waters, gliding over gentle, undulating waves. Our water flight was so peaceful that I completely forgot the apparition on the shore.

Only later, when we splashed onto the beach, did the memory come back to me. I looked about fearfully for the demon, but it was nowhere in sight.

Undine climbed onto a dark, slippery rock. I

joined her, and we lay in silence together, staring up at a great bank of clouds moving swiftly across the sun. Shadows swept over us like giant winged birds. We were dark, then bright; windblown, then caressed.

Undine finally broke the silence. "Did you see them?" she asked.

"Them?"

"There were two under the waves," she said. "One was very large and had many arms."

I sat up and looked at her. She continued to lie on her back, her eyes closed against the sunlight. "Do you mean a giant squid?"

"Perhaps. The other was very long with a thick head, a sorrowful mouth, and teeth like knives."

"A shark?"

"Perhaps."

I took a deep breath. "We swam with these monsters?"

"Monsters? No," she stated simply.

"They—they did not frighten you?" I said.

"No. I think we would not make a good supper for

them. They look for those who are more like themselves."

I sighed. "It seems you are afraid of nothing."

She smiled.

"Not even the demon that haunts this shore?" I asked.

Her eyes opened, and she stared at me calmly. "No. It will not hurt me, either," she said. "I believe it wants to take care of me."

Her words amazed me. "Why do you think a demon would want to take care of you?"

"I do not know." She spoke as simply as if I had asked her opinion of the weather.

"Do you imagine a mortal man might want to take care of you also?" I said.

She laughed softly. "However could he?"

"Perhaps in his world, he could. A civilized world. A world such as mine."

She sat up and leaned close to me. Her cheeks were rosy with sunlight, her eyes glistened.

"I imagine your world is not terribly different from the sea," she said.

"Oh, but it is," I said. "You probably would not like the great crowds of people."

"I should not mind. Not if all the people were like you," she said.

"What am I like?"

"Like"—she seemed to choose her words carefully—"like a big, tame, floppy fish." She laughed softly again; then her lips touched my cheek as gently as a butterfly clings to the bark of a tree.

I tried to embrace her, but she slipped away and ran quickly up the slope, back to the fisherman's hut.

Six

In the afternoon, Undine worked in the garden. I roamed the island, all the while listening for the sound of her hoe breaking up the earth. She was my axis: whether I was brushing my horse or whittling my bow, I located my heart with her.

But soon a thick fog moved in and spread its mantle over the land, and she disappeared. I could no longer hear her working in her garden. I felt bereft.

Then something struck my cheek. Soft and delicate. A violet. Another and another. I turned to look and caught my breath—Undine was tossing violets at me.

"Did you think I was a ghost?" she said.

"Are you?" I said.

"No. So you must not be afraid."

"I am not afraid. I only wish to be your friend, and it grieves me that you have no need for my friendship."

"Why do you say that?"

"Because you are friends with the wind and thunder, with the ocean at midnight—even with monsters in the deep."

"But it is not the same, Lord Huldbrand," she said softly.

"Undine," I breathed. I pulled her close to me.

"You may love me," she said.

I held her tightly and pressed my mouth against hers. As we clung to each other, I wished she would stay with me forever. But then I heard the demon's eerie laughter rippling from the woods. I pulled back in fright, and Undine slipped away, vanishing into the mist, leaving me alone.

"Undine!" I cried.

My cry was answered only by the sound of the gurgling stream. Perhaps I had imagined the demon's laughter. Why did I sense its ghostly presence whenever I drew close to her?

I ran to the fisherman's hut and threw open the door. Undine was sitting calmly with her mother. She stared at me with an impenetrable gaze. Did she want me to show more courage?

I withdrew from her and went back outside. I stumbled down to the sea, until I came upon the fisherman hauling in his nets. "Let me help you," I said.

"'Tis not work for a lord."

"Indeed it is my work if I choose! I am not afraid of honest work, my friend."

He handed me the coarse gray hemp, and I pulled a mass of silver-tinted, speckled fish onto the pebbly shore. As I gripped one and sliced into its glistening pink belly, a violet tumbled from my hair.

 Seven

That evening a gale rocked the island, and one raged inside me as well. I tried to avoid gazing directly at Undine for fear I would betray my obsession with her. But still I was aware of her every movement, her breathing, her scent.

When she stepped out of the hut, I stood by the door and watched her vanish into the rain. I waited, anxious for her return.

When I could bear the strain no longer, I left the hut and walked down the slope in search of her. I called her name, but my voice was lost to the savage breath of the wind.

Finally I came upon her standing at the edge of the sea, staring at the crashing waves. I moved to her, and we stood silently together. The wind nearly blew us over, lightning flashed, and thunder shook the heavens and shore. But with Undine at my side, I felt a part of the wild; we were invincible.

Then I heard a moaning. Peering down the beach, I saw a man lying not far away. It was a bearded man dressed in the dark robes of a priest.

We rushed to him. Undine fell to her knees and lifted his head. As she spoke softly in his ear, his eyes opened and he smiled as if he had been rescued by an angel.

Together we helped the priest to his feet, then led him up the hill to shelter.

We opened the door of the hut and steered the battered man inside. The fisherman rushed to help us. His wife covered her mouth and stared with dark, terrified eyes.

I closed and bolted the door.

"Lean on me, Father," said the fisherman. "Come, we will get you dry clothing." As he helped the priest to the back of the hut, rain dripped from the man's long white beard and black robe.

Undine washed mud and sand from the priest's face, while the fisherman and I removed his sopping robes. I offered my scarlet mantle, but he preferred the fisherman's tattered shawl. We tucked the gray wool around the priest's frail shoulders; then the fisherman led him to the hearth where Undine served him a bowl of broth.

"Tell me, Father," I said once he was settled before the fire. "Where are you from? How did you happen to be washed onto this shore?"

"I was sailing from St. Martin to a village in the north," he said, his voice hoarse. "I was traveling to conduct a wedding there."

"And what happened?"

"I do not know. When I set off this afternoon, the sky was clear, but as I sailed near your shore, I was caught in a sudden tempest, and my sails were ripped to tatters. The vessel was tossed about in the waves until I was thrown into the sea. I was drowning when—" He broke off, coughing.

The fisherman offered his flask, and the priest's

knotted hands shook as he helped himself to the wine, spilling some on his white beard.

"And what happened, Father?" said the fisherman. "How did you get here?"

"Some—some mysterious power seemed to lift me from the waves and drop me onto your shore."

His description startled me; it was not unlike the way I myself had been forced through the dark woods to the fisherman's peninsula.

"What was this power, Father?" I asked. "Do you think it was an evil one?"

"If it was evil, I cannot explain why it delivered me to the warmth of your fire."

"Perhaps it was a good power then," said Undine, "like the power of the sea."

I stared at her. She looked defiantly at all of us, as if she were defending her beloved.

"Whatever it was," said the priest, "I thank Heaven for saving me."

"It was a miracle indeed," said the fisherman. "We are the only inhabitants of this shore for many leagues."

The wind howled, hammering at the shutters.

"A miracle, yes," said the priest, "but for what purpose?"

"I believe I know," said Undine. Her piercing gaze rested on me again, and she lowered her voice to a silvery whisper, "You wish to marry me, do you not, Lord Huldbrand?"

I stared at her, struck speechless by her question. I could not imagine she would choose to leave her wild, enchanted shore to live with me forever.

She misunderstood my hesitation. "Perhaps I am mistaken," she said.

Afraid that she might slip away, I quickly spoke. "Yes," I said. "I do. Reverend sir, would you marry this maiden and me?"

Undine's mother let out a sad cry. But the fisherman spoke up at once. "Yes, Holy Father!" he said. "Please marry our daughter and Lord Huldbrand tonight."

The old woman wept but did not protest. Surely Undine's parents loved their daughter greatly. But perhaps they wanted her to break free from this primitive life and move to a more civilized world.

"Do you answer yes to my proposal?" I asked Undine.

She smiled at me. "I believe you have just answered yes to mine," she said softly.

"Well, then," said the priest, clearing his throat, "let us prepare a wedding ceremony. We need holy candles." The fisherman's wife took two tapers from the cupboard and handed them to the priest.

"And do you have rings, my lord?" the priest said.

"I have no rings, Father."

"What of your chain? Perhaps we can loosen two links from your gold chain?"

"Yes—"

"No, that is not necessary," said Undine. "I have these." She opened her fist, and I caught my breath, for two golden rings glittered in her palm.

"Praise God!" said the fisherman.

"Are you a sorceress?" said the priest, his eyes frightened.

"No," she said. "I found them washed up on the shore after the storm."

The fisherman and priest looked at her with

disbelief. But I regarded this miracle as a sign that we should be united. "Please, marry us now, Father," I said.

The priest seemed reluctant to take his eyes off Undine.

"Now, Father," I said firmly.

He turned away and lit the tapers. And as the wind howled outside and white moths danced about the candle flames, he began intoning the wedding prayer: "Let this woman be wise and faithful. Let her be sober through truth—"

The window shutters flew open, and a cold rainy gust blew out the candles.

Lit only by the dim glow of the hearth, the priest continued: "Let her be venerable through modesty and wise through the teaching of Heaven."

He gave me the kiss of peace, and I passed it on to Undine.

"You may wear your rings now," he said.

As the storm wind blew through the open window, Undine slipped one golden band onto her finger and the other onto mine. They fit perfectly.

"I now pronounce you husband and wife."

The fisherman moved to close the shutters.

"I thought you said you were the only inhabitants of this region," the priest said to him.

"What do you mean?"

"Through the window, just now, while I said the blessing, I saw a figure outside—dressed in white—"

The old woman shrieked and grabbed Undine.

I grabbed my sword, but before I could bolt outside, the fisherman blocked my path.

"Stay! It is gone," he said. "It will not cross our threshold. And tomorrow, when the sun is up, you will leave. The priest will travel with you and bless your way." The fisherman took Undine's hand and placed it in mine. "You must take our daughter away from here. Forever."

Tears streamed down his craggy face. But he wiped them fiercely, then yanked a reed pipe from his pocket and began to play a simple, haunting tune.

The storm ended.

Undine and I lay together on a pile of skins in a simple stall at the back of the hut. Silently we clung to each other, as she swam beneath me in a pool of moonlight. I embraced her nearly all the night. But when she finally fell asleep, I stared at her calm, lovely face and she seemed lost to me. I felt too shy even to touch her.

When I could bear my solitude no longer, I rocked Undine's shoulder. She opened her eyes and stared at me in the moonlight.

"You will miss the sea," I whispered. "Are you certain you want to come with me? Do you want to stay by this shore a while longer?"

"No, I must go now," she said. "Or I am afraid I will never be able to leave."

"Why?"

She sighed. "If I keep swimming farther and farther into the sea, one day I will not come back."

"You fear you will drown?"

"No. I fear I will become a sea creature myself."

I stroked her long, soft hair. "Then I will follow you and swim with you," I said.

She laughed softly. "As long as you love me, we will both be safe, Huldbrand," she whispered.

Her words touched me. "And if I should cease to love you?" I teased.

She did not answer at once. When she did, her voice was more sorrowful than playful. "I cannot imagine what would happen to me," she said.

I pulled her to me and whispered, "Do not even try to imagine such a thing." I kissed her again and again.

In the dark woods, a night bird screamed.

 Eight

The next morning, the flood waters had receded, and only a timid stream meandered about the bottom of the fisherman's land. My horse stamped the dry grass as a yellow butterfly fluttered about his glossy black mane.

Her father's tattered shawl wrapped around her, Undine spoke gently to her mother, soothing her. I stood nearby, speaking with the fisherman.

"After I have completed business with the duke," I said, "we will journey from St. Martin to my castle. You and your wife must come to Ringstetten and visit us."

The old man barely nodded. I wondered if such a

journey might be beyond his imagination. "Take heed in the woods, my lord," he said. "Do not stray from the priest. Let him lead you and bless the way."

"Of course," I said.

"And, my lord—" He gripped my arm tightly and pulled me some distance away from the others. "Once you have left the woods, still you must beware," he said.

"Beware of what?"

"Of the unknown," he said.

I looked at him, startled.

"We do not know where Undine comes from," he said.

"What do you mean?"

"She believes she is our natural child. She does not know the truth, my lord."

"What truth?"

"Eighteen years ago we found her on our threshold. Someone had abandoned her there."

I looked at Undine. She was lovely in the sunlight as she spoke gently to the fisherman's wife, murmuring in her ear. "You have never told her this?" I said.

"No, I confess we want her to believe she is our

daughter. We have loved her desperately. We could never have children of our own."

"But you have no idea where she came from?"

"No—" He glanced about cautiously. "But I must also tell you this: the demon began haunting our shore soon after she arrived."

I felt chilled by his words. "Why? Why do you think it appeared then?"

"I can only believe Undine prompted Evil to crawl out of its lair," he said. When I started to protest, he rushed on. "I am not speaking against her, my lord— she is completely good and innocent. In truth, she is so perfect that I believe the darkness could not bear for us to have her all to ourselves. So it crept forward to watch her, and all these years has waited for her."

I took a deep breath and glanced at Undine again.

"Please protect her, my lord," he said.

"Of course," I breathed.

"Be patient with her. She has lived a very simple life. She does not know the ways of finer folk." Tears started down his grooved cheeks. "*Love her,* my lord," he whispered. "Love her well."

"Yes, of course I will."

A flock of crows swooped down to the grass. Their wings shone blue-black in the early light. A cloud covered the sun.

The shifting shadows seemed to startle the fisherman. "Go now!" he said. He moved away from me to Undine and her mother. He gently separated the two and bade Undine mount my horse.

I took the reins, and on foot I began to lead Undine away from her home. The old woman's voice rose to a howl. The fisherman hid his face behind his worn cap.

Undine looked back at her parents and called out that she loved them.

The priest moved ahead of us, and as we followed him down the slope, I felt chilled by the old woman's shrieks and by the woods that awaited us.

Lifting his robes, the priest waded through the shallow stream. The smell of pine filled the air as we moved beyond the swaying willows. The dark green forest blocked out nearly all the sun, but here and there a shaft of light shot through the branches, threatening to reveal some horror on our path.

I glanced at Undine. She stared ahead at the forest, her face drawn with sorrow. Who was she? Had her real mother abandoned her at the fisherman's hut one night? Perhaps she had been cast onto the shore by a marauding pirate crew who had slain her parents. Whatever her mystery, I imagined tragedy was at its core.

I tried to banish her sorrow by talking of our days ahead. "The duke's castle at St. Martin is the most lavish estate in the kingdom," I said.

I went on to describe the tournament grounds, the gardens, the chapel, and great hall. Undine listened with a grave, almost melancholy expression, and I wondered if she was frightened by the prospect of entering a new world.

But whenever the branches rustled, it was I who jumped in fear. Still, no demon appeared. The woods were quiet, except for the priest murmuring his prayers.

"I am eager to show you my estate also," I said. "The towers of my palace rise so high they nearly touch the heavens."

She smiled as if she could easily see through my attempt to lift her spirits.

"Undine," I confessed, holding her with my gaze, "my castle needs much work, for I have let many things go unattended. I have been restless and have not stayed at home very much in the past few years. But now we will change all that—we shall air out the rooms and fill them with fresh flowers, and plant new trees and restore the fountain. I promise we will make a wonderful home together."

Her eyes seemed to grow brighter.

"And I will love you in every part of our home," I said, "in the midnight garden, on the meadows, near the river, in our bedchambers." As she smiled at me, I wished we were alone, so I could pull her close.

"Lord Huldbrand," the priest called.

I handed Undine the reins of my horse and caught up with him.

"Say your prayers, my lord," he said urgently. "Pray to banish the wickedness that surrounds us."

I wondered if he was referring to my passionate

whispers, but he rushed on. "Something inhuman is near now," he said. "I feel it."

Fear gripped me. Indeed the woods felt colder and more clammy now. My horse neighed in panic.

I turned in time to see the specter loom in the air behind Undine. She smiled at me, unaware of its presence as it spread its ghostly cloak behind her. Its black mouth leered in a white mask of skin.

I shrieked, and my horse galloped out of the demon's reach. I yanked out my sword and rushed like a madman after the phantom as it disappeared behind the trees.

"Huldbrand!" shouted Undine.

I charged deeper into the woods, racing after the phantom. I saw it slip behind a boulder. I followed, and a waterfall gushed over the side of the rock, knocking me to the ground.

I crawled away from the torrent. Soaked and battered, I saw that the monster had vanished.

Suddenly I was afraid for Undine, for I imagined the demon had tricked me into leaving her side so it could now claim her. I rushed back through the forest.

But to my great relief, I found her standing with the priest, unharmed. "What happened?" she said. "Where did you go?"

I glanced at the priest but could not discern whether or not he also had seen the evil apparition.

"I—I thought I saw a thief, a bandit," I said. "Let us proceed quickly." I helped her back into the saddle. Then I took hold of the reins.

"Say your prayers, Father, please," I commanded.

Murmuring softly, the priest walked ahead of us, leading the way through the forest.

Was it my imagination, or did an eerie wail waft through the woods? Tree branches quaked as if some invisible form sobbed against them, weeping out its heart.

Gripping my sword, I dared the spirit who mourned in the shadows to try to steal my bride.

Together, the prayers of the priest and my resolve kept the demon at bay. By the time we reached the edge of the woods, the gloom had lifted. Birds sang beyond the dark trees.

Stepping into an open field of barley, we were

bathed in the warm light of the afternoon sun, and such incredible relief washed over me that I began to laugh. My laughter celebrated my life: my castle at Ringstetten, all my tournaments, hunts, feasts, and daily concerns. We were safe now, completely safe.

I was startled when I turned and saw Undine astride my horse. Staring at the spires of the duke's castle looming in the distance, she seemed a mirage from a dark dream world, not a part of this sun-bright, ordinary world, the world I had left behind when I met her. For a moment I felt a disturbing distance between us.

"My lord—" The priest touched my shoulder. "I must leave you now," he said. "My monastery rests on a hill this side of the duke's castle."

I bade him good luck and farewell. Then he somberly raised his hand and blessed Undine and me. He started to leave, then turned back. "Call for me if you should ever need me, Lord Huldbrand," he said. Perhaps he sensed we had not fully escaped the forest's evil.

I tried to lighten his mood. "I hope we shall call upon you to celebrate a christening someday soon, my friend," I said.

But no smile answered mine. The priest simply turned and left us.

Lonely music wafted from a shepherd's flute. I looked back at Undine. She clutched her shawl and stared at the barley field. Did the rippling silver-gold grain remind her of her ocean waves? Was she yearning for the sound of the fisherman's pipe? For a terrible moment, I regretted having stolen her from her old life.

Then the fisherman's words came back to me. He had begged me to take Undine far away from the inhuman force haunting their shore. Revived by the memory of his charge, I began leading my horse through the swelling fields.

Evening bells chimed. We arrived in the square of St. Martin, then moved down a path between rows of peasant cottages with steeply gabled roofs, past old men and women grinning toothlessly, skinny dogs barking, and ragged children waving and calling to us.

The castle gong sounded as we entered the outer ward of the duke's estate.

We moved past the rambling thatched-roof stables

and the mews filled with shrieking falcons. By the time we had passed the tournament grounds with their cheerful red banners flapping in the breeze, I had nearly forgotten our nightmarish journey.

Stable boys caught sight of us and called to one another. A smithy left off shoeing a horse. Maids abandoned milk pails and joined the oxherds who followed us through the twilight.

I led my horse toward the inner ward. We approached the gate towers, and the watchman began blowing the great horn from the turret, announcing the arrival of Lord Huldbrand and his bride.

 Nine

Undine hardly spoke in the hours following our arrival. As lanterns flickered in our chambers in the west wing of the duke's palace, she sat near the window and stared into the dark.

I imagined the luxury of her new surroundings made her weary: the high, canopied bed with its damask curtains, the arched windows with their leaden panes, the dark-paneled walls, painted ceiling, and tallow lamps.

I moved to her side and spoke quietly. "Forgive me. I know you must be lonely. This life is so different from yours. I know you must long for the sea."

"I can hear the waves," she said softly.

I could almost hear them myself. "I know," I said. "Let them stay in your heart. But perhaps you will also grow to love the sounds of your new world. Do you hear the music in the garden? Someone is playing a lute. Someone is planning a feast."

As she stared silently out the window, I stroked her hair, and we listened together to the garden music and the gentle speech rising from below.

Soon she began repeating words we heard, as if learning the lyrics to a new song: *satin, sugarplums, peacocks, lavender, jugglers, spiced wine, garlands, hyssop, pennyroyal.*

Early the next morning, I set out alone to conduct my affairs with the duke. I was eager to finish our meeting so I could spend time with Undine—show her about the castle.

Sitting opposite me, the dignified, white-haired gentleman slowly discussed the purchasing of sheep from my estate. I tried to speed the conference along, but he was quite measured in his deliberations as he went on to review the expenditures of my wine and wool trade. Eventually, his steward interrupted us to report a quarrel between two of his woodcutters.

I took advantage of the intrusion to beg my leave. Before the duke would let me go, however, he insisted that Undine and I stay for several days. "My daughter Bertalda is quite excited about your visit," he said. "I fear she has been terribly lonely since her sister left home. In fact, she is preparing a banquet to honor your marriage, so you must at least stay for that event."

I accepted the duke's invitation, then quickly hurried back to our chambers. When I entered our room, the silence was palpable. Undine was gone. I rushed into the hall and called to a servant, but he did not know where she was.

Unreasonably, I feared she had fled the castle. Perhaps in my absence she had come to regret her decision to leave the sea after all.

I hurried to the courtyard and questioned the kitchen helpers on their way to the great hall. I asked the young maids drawing water from the well. No one had seen her.

As I searched the grounds, I heard her laughter.

Rounding the garden hedge, I saw her sitting on a wooden bench at the edge of a pale green lawn. Another maiden held her hand and spoke earnestly to her. I recognized the fair-haired young woman to be the duke's youngest daughter, Lady Bertalda.

Lady Bertalda spied me and waved. "Welcome, Lord Huldbrand!" she called in a pleasant, cultured voice. "I kidnapped your lovely wife from your chambers and brought her down to the garden. I beg your mercy."

I approached and kissed Bertalda's hand, declaring my forgiveness.

"Thank you," she said. "Please sit down and join us. Undine was telling me about the wild plants that grow near her father's house. I believe she has just described blue sea holly, lovage, and gold poppy." She turned back to Undine. "I have only bought them in the marketplace. I have never seen them growing in the wild."

In times past I had found Lady Bertalda very appealing, with her kind features and flaxen braids entwined with ribbons. But sitting beside Undine now, she seemed pale and ordinary.

She looked at me again and exclaimed, "Perhaps Undine and I can go together to our fields, and I will show her all the healing plants in this region."

"Of course," I said. "It seems we will be staying here for a few days. We are looking forward with great pleasure to your feast."

"Oh, wonderful!" Lady Bertalda turned back to Undine. "We are having a great feast in honor of your marriage, and I plan to give you my most beautiful gown to wear. It has just arrived from the looms of Cathay. It is wine-colored with silver stars. And the fair has just come to town! So we will have dancers and jugglers and mimes—"

"Mimes?" said Undine.

"Yes, mimes," I explained. "They play with invisible things—tell stories without speaking."

"Like this," said Bertalda. She pretended to toss a ball to me, and I pretended to catch it and throw it back.

Undine laughed, prompting Bertalda to toss the

imaginary ball to her. But Undine pretended to miss it. She dashed after it, scooped it off the grass, and gracefully tossed it to me.

As I caught the imaginary ball high in the air and hurled it to Bertalda, Undine's silver laughter woke up the placid garden, shaking the leaves of the chestnuts and scattering robins from the grass.

Ten

For the next few days, Undine helped Bertalda prepare for the feast. The activity about the castle was astonishing: housemaids wove chaplets of flowers for the guests; serving boys cut lilies and mint to spread over the floor of the great hall. Acrobats, jugglers, and mimes rehearsed their acts. Hunters returned with fresh boar, venison, and rabbit; fishermen delivered trout, pike, bream, and mackerel; pigs were slaughtered and trussed, along with geese, hens, and peacocks.

Weaving in and out of all the activity was Undine. She made garlands of gillyflowers and marigolds. She applauded the mimes practicing near the well and visited the musicians in the great hall. She moved like quicksilver from castle to courtyard to garden, as if she were only visiting this earth for a short while, as if she had to catch it all, marvel at the things of this world now. And when she was near, the jugglers tossed their oranges higher; viol players played more passionately; maidens sang their rounds with more joy.

On the night of the banquet, a blast of trumpets announced our arrival in the great hall. Undine and I took seats of honor on the dais next to the duke and his family. As we sat on carved, canopied chairs at the oaken table, boar hounds stood proudly by.

Undine held my hand, and she and Bertalda talked together and laughed until finally the bishop called for silence. After he said grace, another blast of the trumpets brought a slew of servants into the hall, bearing silver trays laden with suckling pigs, peacocks, pheasants, and partridges.

A second flank paraded in with trout, herring, shad, rice, baked apples, pears, sugarplums, almonds, and walnuts. Cupbearers poured sparkling wines and champagnes.

"Undine! Look!" Bertalda cried out.

Two squires were bringing forth an enormous pie. They set it before Undine and handed her a large carving knife. She stared at it with confusion as everyone in the hall watched her.

"Cut it very gently, Undine," said Bertalda, "along the edges, then lift off the crust."

Undine carved gingerly around the mountainous pastry. When she lifted off the crust, a flock of blackbirds flew out. The room rang with laughter and cheers as the birds rose toward the high vaulted ceiling. My gaze followed their flight, until I froze with horror.

High up, in one of the balconies of the hall, was a specter. The being seemed to be staring straight at our table, its black eyes set deep in a ghostly white face. Its inhuman gaze penetrated my heart as keenly as an arrow.

"Huldbrand!" said Undine, laughing. "Did you know they were there?"

"What?" I looked at her, dazed with horror.

"The birds . . ." The smile left her face. "What is it?"

I could not answer. Fear clouded my gaze; I looked at her blindly.

She touched my face. "Huldbrand, are you all right?"

"Yes, yes," I said, forcing a smile. "I am fine, my love." I put my arm around her and clutched her to me as I looked back at the balcony.

The demon had vanished.

Where had it gone? Had it escaped to the shadowy passageways? To our chambers? Or was it everywhere?

 Eleven

I do not know how I got through the next hours. I tried to behave with decorum but kept casting a frantic eye about the great hall. Had the demon been a hallucination? Perhaps in the dark woods the horrific image had so branded itself on my mind that it had momentarily been resurrected as a mirage, a waking dream. Or—as I truly believed—had the ghost followed us? Was it now hiding somewhere in the duke's castle, lurking in the shadows, waiting for the chance to capture my wife?

I kept Undine close to me for the rest of the feast, then steered her back to our chambers, mindful of every shadow and every movement.

Undine asked several times if I was all right, and each time I answered that I was only a bit weary.

I bolted our door. Once Undine was asleep, I did not blow out the lamp, but lay awake, alert and anxious, guarding her. I made the decision that we should leave St. Martin tomorrow. As soon as dawn broke, I would tell her.

But when the wind gusted through the window and I jumped with fear, she woke. "Huldbrand, what is the matter?"

"Nothing. Go back to sleep."

"No. You must tell me what worries you."

The breeze stirred the curtains again; I glanced sharply at the window. "Nothing," I whispered. "I only want you to be safe—safe and happy in your new life."

"Oh, you must not worry about me," she whispered. "I am more able to take care of myself than most of the knights in the duke's realm."

In one way she was right—she could swim the ocean and wander the night with more courage than any soldier. But what defense did she have against a ghost?

"I know," I said, kissing her hair. "But I imagine all

the world might want to steal you from me. I will be less worried when we return to Ringstetten tomorrow."

"Tomorrow? But I should like to visit Bertalda longer. There are so many things we want to do together—search for plants and go to the fair—"

"Forgive me," I interrupted, "but we must return to my castle. I have important business there."

"Oh, but I love her, Huldbrand," she said. "I scarcely know her, but I love her. Besides you, she is the first friend I have ever had. Please, I do not want to leave her right away."

"I promise you this," I said, "Lady Bertalda will visit us very soon. You will not be separated from her for long. But we have no choice. We must leave tomorrow."

Lady Bertalda seemed as distressed as Undine when we sat with her in the garden and shared our intention to leave.

"But I have barely had time to know you," she said, clutching Undine's hand.

"You shall know her better," I assured her, "for you must come soon to visit us at Ringstetten."

"Yes, very soon," Undine said.

"I should like that," said Bertalda. She did not let go of Undine's hand as she led us into the castle and ordered a carriage for our journey and bade servants load it with gowns, fabrics, fur coverlets, tapestries, spices, fruits, and flowers.

Soon my horse was tied to the back of the carriage, footman and driver were in place, and Undine and I were ensconced among roses, furs, and silks.

As we waved goodbye to Bertalda and the duke, my eye caught a tall figure watching us from the crowd. The face was hidden; the figure was shrouded in a white cloak. I gasped.

"Huldbrand, what is it?" said Undine.

Just then the wind blew the cloak and the hood fell away, revealing the craggy and sun-weathered face of an old man.

"Nothing," I said. "It is nothing."

But as we rode off, he continued to stare after us, his eyes the color of seawater.

 Twelve

The journey to Ringstetten took almost the entire day. As our carriage proceeded up the hill toward the walled fortress of my castle, hundreds of noisy birds fluttered about the trees lining the road.

Breathing in the scent of lilac and honeysuckle, I felt at ease for the first time in weeks. From now on we would be safe. No ghosts inhabited this familiar, friendly realm. The nightmares of the recent past seemed worlds away as we rode through the great gate and heard the gleeful voices of servants rushing to greet us.

Word of my marriage had traveled before us, and as we stepped from the carriage, children offered Undine garlands of flowers. In the soft twilight, she embraced the boys and girls, and they kissed her cheeks and stroked her rippling hair as if they'd known her always.

I finally led her away from the admiring throng toward my palace. Once we had slipped inside the dark vestibule, I pulled her to me. "Welcome to your new home," I whispered. "We will have a good life here. I promise."

In the cool, damp air, she encircled me with her arms. "Yes, we will, as long as you stay close to me," she said.

"Close?" I chuckled, holding her tightly in the blackness. "We are so close, I cannot even see you."

For the next two days, I gave Undine tours of her new home. We visited the stables, mews, kitchen, smithy, granary; we rode over the countryside, surveying farms and woodlands. My steward, butler, stable hands, falconers, blacksmiths, overseer, chamberlain, cook, maids, and gardeners all seemed to adore her, and in her presence they stood taller, laughed more heartily, and spoke more cheerfully than I had ever seen them do.

On the third morning after our return, I felt compelled to attend to the business of Ringstetten, so I left Undine in the company of her new handmaidens and went to my meeting hall.

My first order of business was to call for my gardener and order him to uncover the fountain in the center of the courtyard.

"But the spring waters dried up last year, my lord," he said. "I doubt the fountain will ever flow again."

"Please do what you can," I urged him. "I want everything on my estate to be fertile and alive."

"Very well." He smiled, guessing, I supposed, that Undine inspired me.

I even seemed to please my grumpy chamberlain when I requested the cleaning and airing of all the castle rooms. "Ah, it is about time!" he said. "A man living alone keeps a terrible house. Now it will be different, finally!"

I met with overseers and directed the replenishing of livestock and the planting of new apple and pear seedlings in the summer orchard. In the afternoon, I met with my steward, and we discussed the recent sale of my wine and wool at the market of St. Martin.

At twilight when I was reviewing my account sheets, I glanced out the window overlooking the courtyard and observed with disappointment that my gardener had been right: the spring was still dry. The uncovered fountain did not give forth even a trickle.

At that moment Undine and a handmaiden emerged from the castle. Though the day was still quite hot, Undine looked lovely and serene in a long linen gown. Her hair was loose and blew softly in the wind.

I was about to call to her, but then I became distracted by the fountain. Water had begun to soak the ground. The flow grew stronger and stronger, bubbling up into the air, until the torrent was quite magnificent.

I could hardly believe what was happening. The waters seemed to be sentient, leaping and dancing in the twilight. Then to my astonishment, Undine stepped directly under the cascade and let the fountain waters rain down on her, soaking her hair and gown and slippers.

Standing in the waters, she seemed to shimmer with an unearthly pink radiance. Her handmaiden stared at her mistress, her face reflecting the delight and yearning for the wild I myself felt—the same emotion I had known watching Undine swim in the sea. Glittering in the fountain, she looked like a sea goddess from a mythical time.

 Thirteen

Early the next day, Undine and I breakfasted on cheese and fresh baked bread in the garden. Birds flew across a sky as blue as cathedral glass, and goose girls drove honking geese into the silvery wet meadow below us where woolly sheep dotted the horizon.

"Beyond that meadow and beyond the cedar forest is the Black River," I explained. "Later this afternoon, perhaps we can go there together. But now I must travel to court. While I am gone, you should begin to supervise the household."

"How do I do that?" she asked.

"You direct the spinning and weaving and—"

"I cannot direct anyone, Huldbrand."

"Well, then, simply tour the grounds and the castle—tell them they are all doing splendid jobs."

She smiled.

"Visit the kitchen; compliment the cook. Give a good word to the chambermaids; ask them to sprinkle dried roses in all the closets."

"Lovely," she said.

"Tell the gardeners to prepare sand for the hourglasses." I kissed her hand and stood. "And you must visit the steward and arrange alms for the poor."

It was midafternoon when I returned from court. I stabled my horse and hastened to find Undine. But when I came to our chambers, her maid told me she had left the castle that morning. "She said she was going to the river, my lord. She has not returned."

It troubled me that she had gone to the river without me. "No one accompanied her?"

"No, she would not allow it. She said she would find her way."

As I rode across the field, the dark green cedar forest was silhouetted against the gray sky. At the meadow's edge, I dismounted and made my way between the trees, traveling the footpath that led down to the river. The air of the forest was alive with birdsong, insect chirping, and the gurgling sounds of water. Tender shoots of new plants, white star-shaped flowers, and pale green mosses carpeted the ground.

When I came to the river's edge, I found no sign of Undine. I imagined she might be swimming, sunbathing on a rock, or collecting plants near the water. I traipsed through the reeds and cattails looking for her.

Then I heard her laughter. I started to call out, but stopped, for I heard the laughter of another, deep and resonant.

Undine and a stranger emerged from behind a thicket. Both were clad in white—she in her bleached linen gown and he in a white hooded cloak.

He saw me first and stopped. I stared at his sunweathered, craggy face and his pale eyes, and I could not breathe.

"Huldbrand!" Undine ran toward me along the bank, her wet gown clinging to her legs. I was trembling as she put her arms around me and kissed me. When I looked past her, the stranger was gone. "Who was he?" My voice sounded strangled.

"Oh—" She turned to look for the man. "Where did he go? His name is Kuhleborn. He said he is a hermit who lives in these woods."

"No," I said. "I've seen him before, but not here."

"Where did you see him?"

"In the courtyard at the duke's castle—the day we left St. Martin."

"Really?"

"I will send my soldiers to find him." My heart was racing.

"Your soldiers? Why?"

I did not answer as I turned and began moving back along the riverbank.

"Huldbrand!" Undine caught up to me. "I think he means no harm."

"Why do you defend him?" I shouted, whirling on her.

She stepped back. "I do not defend him," she said,

eyeing me with a calm, steady gaze. "I do not even know him. We met only a moment ago when I was gathering pebbles."

I looked down the bank, furious and frightened, hoping to see the intruder again, yet dreading I might.

"Why are you so afraid?" she said.

"I am not afraid. I am angry. He is trespassing on my land! What have you been doing all day? Why did you come here without me?"

"I came to visit the river. I wanted to be near the water, Huldbrand."

"Well, you should not have come here by yourself. It is dangerous."

"I do not believe I was in danger, Huldbrand. And I will come back here alone. I must."

"Why?" I asked angrily.

"Because I think I could grow to love the river as deeply as I love the sea. I have missed the water, Huldbrand." She slipped her hand into mine, and the touch of her skin cooled my anger. "Please, do not try to keep me from it."

I sighed. "Of course. You may swim here, if you like," I said.

But then I looked away from her, back at the river-bank. "Later I will come back," I said, more to myself than to her. "I will find that man again—and learn exactly who he is."

Fourteen

I could not stop thinking about the old man. I was certain I had seen him at the duke's castle the morning we had left. But how could he possibly be the same person? Had he followed us from St. Martin to Ringstetten? These questions tormented me through dinner. As soon as Undine went off to visit some servant children, I seized the opportunity to return to the river.

The sky was growing dark as I left my horse at the edge of the woods and hurried toward the water. Following the path that led along the river, I kept an eye out for the hermit. The flowing water sounded ominous; the bird cries and insect chirpings seemed more like warnings than friendly summer song. But there was no sign of anyone.

I was about to turn back when I saw a white figure in the distance. Kuhleborn?

I started to shout to him, but then I froze with horror. The white figure was rising into the air. I watched it glide over the water. Then it swirled down into the river. As it disappeared, demonic laughter rippled from the watery vortex.

I stared transfixed as the river resumed its gentle flow. Then I began running back the way I had come. I could scarcely feel my legs beneath me as I trampled the reeds and charged back through the cedar woods.

At the edge of the meadow, I pulled myself onto my horse and spurred him homeward. Galloping through the dusky light, I could hear the phantom's laughter echoing in my ears.

I left my horse at the castle gate and ran across the courtyard, frantic to find Undine. I hurried through the vestibule, then down the long passageway that led to our chambers.

I heard her laughter before I saw her.

My heart beat madly as I neared our door; I caught my breath as I peered into our room. She was kneeling before the hearth, showing her collection of river pebbles to a small servant boy.

My eyes filled with tears as I watched her laugh in the firelight. Perhaps the fisherman had spoken the truth: her beauty and goodness *had* prompted some jealous and mysterious Evil to steal from its shadowland. I felt such pain in my heart I could barely stand.

Later, as Undine slept, I sat alone in the great hall, watching the fire in the hearth. A flame snaked along a log, flared upward, then vanished—only to appear again a moment later. Staring at the elusive fire, I went over recent events in my mind. Was the ghostly spirit by the river the same that had haunted the fisherman's woods? Had it earlier changed its shape to appear as Kuhleborn? And how was it connected to the sudden waterfall . . . and the swirling river?

Exhausted from fear and worry, I finally rose to return to our chambers. But when I stepped into our room, I found Undine was gone. I hurried down the torchlit passageway and called her name, but there was no answer.

I raced to the courtyard, fearing she might already have been stolen from me. I was about to call my guards when I saw her: she was standing in the fountain, eyes closed, her gown lying on the flagstones.

I called her name, but she did not seem to hear me. As the moon-bright waters streamed down her naked body, I was filled with a jealousy I could not explain.

I stepped up to the fountain and grabbed her arm. She cried out as she stumbled toward me.

"Undine!" I shouted, pulling her from the cascade. I snatched her gown from the stones and roughly handed it to her. "Cover yourself, before others see you," I said.

She looked at me, frightened and dazed. "What happened?" She was shivering as she pulled her gown over her wet body.

"I do not remember getting out of bed," she cried in a high voice. "I do not remember anything!"

"Why not? Were you under a spell?" I still felt angry and unreasonably jealous.

"A spell?" She sounded confused. "I do not know, Huldbrand. I cannot remember!"

The fear in her voice softened my anger, and I felt compassion for her. I pulled her to me and held her tightly. "Come, let us return to our chambers before anyone sees you."

I guided Undine back into the palace and down the passageway. When we came to our chambers, I kissed her and said, "I am going to stay up for a while. Please go to bed. Do not wait for me."

I instructed my guards to stand watch outside our chambers. Then I returned to my hall and brooded again before my fire. Near midnight, I made the decision to send for the fisherman and his wife.

I also decided to send for Lady Bertalda, for I imagined her educated, reasonable way of thinking would help Undine. These opposites combined, I thought, might provide a powerful screen between my castle and inhuman forces.

Though it was late, I hurried to my hall and called for two messengers. The first I ordered to the duke's castle and the other to the fisherman's peninsula.

For the remainder of the night, I paced the castle ramparts alone, on the lookout for ghostly trespassers.

 Fifteen

By dawn I had decided to visit the monastery near St. Martin. I wanted to question the priest who had accompanied us through the dark forest.

I told Undine I would return by nightfall. Then after I ordered my guards to watch her all day, I set off for the green hills between Ringstetten and St. Martin.

When I arrived, I found the priest inside the abbey church. Sunlight lit the stained glass behind his head as he prayed before a statue of the Virgin Mary.

I waited until he had finished. When I approached, he did not seem surprised to see me. Without a word, he beckoned me to follow him outside into the garden.

For a few moments, we sat silently under an elm and watched the monks cut the hedges and scythe the grass. Finally I spoke. "Father, I have seen a terrible sight in my woods."

He nodded and, without looking at me, crossed himself.

"I saw a demon—the same that I saw on our journey through the fisherman's woods," I said.

He watched the grass cutters without expression.

"Father, I fear I am going mad. I must ask you if you saw it also. That day in the forest, did you see the phantom? Did you hear it weep?"

He ran his knotted hand down his long, white beard and nodded slowly.

The bells of the church rang. I waited for them to stop before I went on, "Then tell me, Father, what is it? What?"

He looked at me. "Have you asked your wife, Lord Huldbrand?"

I caught my breath. "She does not know the answer to these questions, Father. She knows only that she has felt the presence of this ghost all her life. She said it seems to watch over her."

"How well do you know your wife, Lord Huldbrand?"

His question startled me. "I know her well. I know she is kind and brave and wise."

"But do you know where she is from?"

I did not want to add fuel to his suspicions, so I lied. "I believe she was born to the fisherman and his wife."

He gave me a penetrating look.

"Where do *you* think she is from, Father?" I said.

"Do not ask me unless you want my honest answer, Lord Huldbrand."

I inhaled sharply. "Where do you think she is from, Father?" I asked again.

"I cannot say exactly. But from the moment she brought forth the gold rings for your wedding ceremony, I have been frightened of her. I began to sense then that she is connected to another world, a world not human."

The church bells rang again. I felt dizzy.

"I fear"—he looked at me and spoke in a hoarse whisper—"I fear the demon in the forest was trying to unite with its own kin."

I recoiled from his words. "I do not understand how you can say such an abominable thing."

He lowered his head. "I cannot explain it, Lord Huldbrand, and I have no evidence and no authority to make such a charge. Forgive me if I am wrong."

I looked away from him and stared at the scythes slashing the tall grass, cutting it into green ribbons. I felt ill as I stood up. "Pray for us, Father," I said. Then I left for the stables.

It was nearly dark when I arrived home. My steward told me Undine was in the meadow, playing with children. I sent for my guards. At first, both seemed reluctant to report on her.

"Where did she go?" I said. "The meadow? The river?"

"We followed her to the river," mumbled one.

"Then what?"

"We watched her," said the other.

"Yes? And what happened? Was anyone there?"

"Aye, my lord. She met an old man there."

"Yes," I whispered, "and he wore a white cloak?"

"Aye, they talked for a bit. Then he must have seen us because he left quickly."

"And what did she do then?" I said.

"She swam in the river, my lord."

"Aye, she swam a long time," said the other, his eyes bright with excitement, "up and down the river, vanishing for long minutes. We feared she'd drowned, but then she appeared again, like a miracle."

"And then what? What did she do after her swim?"

"She came ashore," said one.

"And returned to the castle," said the other.

"Thank you. Thank you very much." I dismissed them and moved swiftly out of my hall and down the narrow passageway to our chambers. A servant told me Undine was still in the meadow.

As I hurried outside and through the courtyard, moonlight rimmed the hedge bordering my grounds. The fountain bubbled wildly, flinging its spray into the wind.

I pushed through the gate and started down the footpath leading from the castle to the meadow. It was dark, and the air was heavy with moisture.

Clouds raced over the full moon. I stumbled and fell. Cursing, I rose and moved more cautiously; rocks and pebbles slid ahead of me. I stopped and caught my breath.

A light rain began to fall. And then I heard the sound of singing—haunting, high-pitched singing, like the singing on the fisherman's shore.

"Undine?" I cried.

The singing stopped. But there was no sign of her, unless she was disguised as the owl hooting from the cedar wood or the distant wolf howling at the moon. At the moment, all the world seemed the product of sorcery.

"Show yourself!" I commanded the dark.

The wind rushed out of the night—a cool, wet wind. I stepped back in horror. Something was rushing toward me—a dark shape. I crouched on the road and covered my head, like a child before a monster.

"Huldbrand!" Undine's voice rang out.

"Yes?" I said, rising from the ground.

She laughed and fell against me. "Look!" she cried. She thrust her fists before my eyes and opened them slowly to reveal two iridescent points of light.

I pushed her hands away and cried, "What is it?"

"Fireflies! I caught them for you."

"My God," I breathed. "Is that all?"

"Yes. Are they not beautiful?"

"Lovely," I whispered.

"Now that you have seen them," she said, "I will set them free." She opened her arms to the night, and the two points of light flickered into the air. They sparked again and again, until they were swallowed up by the rainy blackness.

"Where have you been?" she said. "I have hardly seen you for the last two days."

I moved beyond her reach. "I have had a great deal to do," I said. I felt a bit frightened of her as I started back toward the castle.

"Why are you running from me, Huldbrand?" She caught up with me, and her cool hand wrapped around mine. But I withdrew from her touch.

"I am not running from you. I only want to return home quickly, for I still must go over my accounts," I said.

As I walked through the rain back into my palace, she followed. Without looking at her, I bade her good night outside my hall. Then I escaped to my own quarters.

I sat before my fire and tried to think clearly. Was the priest right—was Undine allied with Kuhleborn? Who was he? Was he a shape-shifter who could assume ghostly forms as well as human?

As I stared out my window at the black night, rain pounded the glass panes; the wind was rising.

"Huldbrand?"

I turned to face Undine: she was standing very still as the flickering light cast shadows across her face. "Why have you grown fearful of me?" she said.

I looked at her for a long moment without speaking, then said coldly, "You met your friend Kuhleborn on the riverbank again today. Did you see him tonight as well?"

"No," she said. "I only spoke with him briefly this afternoon."

"Ah, and what did you speak about?"

"He told me about his life as a sailor."

"A sailor?"

"Yes. He said he had once sailed the seven seas. He said he wanted to tell me about the beauties of the deep."

"Indeed? Well, I should think you would be more cautious with strangers, Undine, since my woods now harbor the demon that is so enamored of you."

She looked stunned. "You have seen it here?" she said.

I realized in that moment that she truly did not know about the phantom. "Forgive me," I breathed. "I did not mean to alarm you."

"But you saw something?" she said.

"Yes," I said. "I saw a white form glide over the river. Then I heard the demon's laughter."

"Oh." She stared directly at me, her eyes glistening in the candlelight. "And now you do not trust me?" she said.

I looked away from her. "I—I feel I do not know you," I said.

"Look at me, Huldbrand."

I looked at her.

"Do you see your enemy here?" she said softly.

I shook my head.

"I do not know why the demon has followed us," she said. "But I do know that if we do not stay close to each other, it will destroy us."

I looked at her for a long moment. The rain was beating against the ground; tree branches scraped the glass. It was a night not unlike our wedding night.

"I am sorry," I said, all my fear of her collapsing. "I did not mean to turn on you. I promise not to forsake you again." I went to her and held her face between my hands. "Please forgive me," I said in a choked voice. I inhaled her sweet scent, felt her soft flesh.

My heart was racing and I felt like weeping. I loved her and I could not fathom who she really was. But her mystery was my fault, not hers; it was my fear of the unknown that kept me from truly knowing her.

 Sixteen

The next morning while I met with my overseer, I heard the gong sound at the bailey gate. Then the watchman blew his horn. From my window, I saw the duke's carriage clatter across the stone courtyard. Lady Bertalda had arrived.

I hurried outside to greet her. "You have come much sooner than I expected!" I cried.

"I left immediately," she said. "Your message seemed urgent."

I quickly made the decision not to share my fears with her. "Urgent only because you were so kind to us," I said, "and we longed to repay your generosity."

A cry rose from the palace entrance. Undine dashed across the stone yard and flew into Bertalda's arms. As I watched the two women greet each other like sisters, my burden felt considerably lighter.

In a short time, Lady Bertalda's energy and common sense helped supplant my fear and dread of the demon apparition and my confusion about Undine. I almost ceased to believe my estate was haunted as Bertalda led us about the castle, graciously suggesting further alterations: she recommended whitewashing the stonework in the courtyard, spreading fresh lilies and mint about our floors, hanging sprigs of fern to collect flies and alder leaves to catch fleas. She unrolled bolts of imported silk and instructed my tailor how to cut a proper sleeve for Undine. She made perfumed water by filling wooden tubs with rose petals and letting them steep all day in the sun.

On the third day of her visit, Bertalda requested an elegant dinner be served beneath the trees, so I sent my squires to invite the nobles from nearby estates.

That evening, our party sat at a long table above

the meadow. Servants held torches as kitchen helpers brought spiced wine, herring pie, and baked apples. Undine and Bertalda's lovely company seemed to inspire the men. Goblets were tipped, and speech and laughter swelled in the waning light.

Just as we finished our dessert, a servant delivered the news that my emissary had returned. I excused myself and went to my hall. There the messenger whom I had sent to the fisherman's coast waited for me. He reported that the fisherman and his wife had refused to come with him. He said they were too frightened to visit their daughter.

"Why are they frightened?" I asked him.

"I do not know, my lord. The old man said he was afraid of something he dared not speak about."

These words sent a chill through me. I dismissed the messenger. Standing at my window, I stared at the fountain in the courtyard. *Beware of the unknown,* the fisherman had told me the morning we had left him. Did he believe what the priest believed—that Undine was not of this world?

With a heavy heart, I returned to my party.

Everyone was now gathered before the stone hearth in the great hall. Bertalda was teaching Undine to embroider, showing her how to work a moon into her cloth. As a knight told a humorous tale about a jousting tournament, all laughed, including Undine. In this moment, in the glow of the fire, she appeared no different from the rest, only perhaps more beautiful, more alive.

These sane, educated gentry who sat before my hearth would be appalled by my worries about the supernatural. Phantoms, mad waters, unholy magic, peasant fears—none were part of a nobleman's thinking. My guests would all assure me that my ghostly visions had been illusions; they might say I had only been witness to river vapor floating in the twilight.

Suddenly the veil of irrational thought fell away. Relief swept over me as I threw myself into the happy conversation. I invited everyone to stay for another day. I promised a good hunt, imported food and wine, games of backgammon and blindman's bluff.

* * *

The next morning, as I had promised, I organized a hawking party for my guests. Hawking was Bertalda's favorite activity; indeed, she had brought the best falcon from her father's mews.

Though Undine had never participated in the sport and seemed to know nothing about it, Bertalda convinced her to come with us. With innocent amazement, Undine stared at the falcons perched on our gloves. And when we set off across the countryside, she rode with us, though a bit behind.

I kept looking back to make certain she was safe as we galloped over the meadow and into the woods. Only when the horn blew and the hounds flushed their game did I momentarily forget her. Our party unhooded our birds and watched them soar into the blue sky, their tiny leg bells tinkling through the summer air.

Once the falcons had slain their prey, we blew our silver whistles and swung our lures, and they flew back to our wrists. The hounds returned with the kill, and we surveyed a good catch—herons, thrushes, cormorants, and quail.

I looked about for Undine, but she was nowhere in sight.

I inquired of the others, but none had seen her. I excused myself and took off hastily across the countryside, anxious to find her. I galloped all the way to the castle gate. There the watchman told me Undine had returned a short time ago.

As I entered the courtyard, I saw her standing by the fountain. I called out her name, but she did not answer. She stood very still and glared at me. "Why do you stare so?" I asked.

"You are murderers," she said.

"What?"

"Murderers. You are all murderers!"

"What are you talking about?"

"You never told me you killed birds for sport— slaughtered them for fun."

"You do not understand," I said.

"I understand they will never fly again; they will never sing." Her eyes filled with tears.

"That is ridiculous!" I exclaimed.

Suddenly the fountain waters roared into the air. Before I could move away, they crashed down on top of me. I fell headlong to the flagstones. As my blood streamed into the waters, I heard the hideous laughter of the phantom.

"Huldbrand!" Undine cried.

I reached for her. But all the world faded to black.

Seventeen

I woke to the sound of rain. I was lying in a shadowed room under a pile of furs. Bertalda sat near me, sewing in the firelight.

I tried to sit up. Bertalda rose from her chair. "Lie down, lie down," she said. She covered my brow with a wet cloth perfumed with rose water.

"What happened?" I asked hoarsely.

"Shhh. Rest now. You have had an accident."

"Why—what happened?"

"You fell on the stones near the fountain."

I tried to sit up again, but the pain in my head was too great. "Where is Undine?" I asked.

"Wandering in the rain. She seems—" Bertalda frowned.

"What? Tell me."

"She seems to have gone a bit mad, Huldbrand."

"What—what do you mean?"

"She keeps walking about the grounds, wringing her hands. For some reason, she believes *she* caused the fountain to hurt you, and she is overwrought with remorse."

"What does she mean, she caused it?"

"I do not know."

"Send her to me, please."

Bertalda went to fetch Undine. A moment later, they stood together in the doorway. Undine looked frightened.

"Come here," I said, reaching out for her.

She moved toward me cautiously, like a hunted animal. Short of my bed, she stopped.

"Come," I insisted. I started to rise, but the pain forced me down.

"Go to him," Bertalda urged her. "Give him your hand."

Undine stepped forward and gave me her cold, wet hand. I gripped it tightly and lay back down. "Please— leave us a moment," I said to Bertalda and her maid.

When they had gone, I asked Undine to sit beside me. "What is the matter with you?" I said.

"I nearly killed you," she whispered.

"No! You did not. What do you mean? It was the fountain, not you."

"But the water did my bidding," she whispered.

"Nonsense! That is madness—superstition. None of us—no human—can determine the flow of the water."

"But I feel I did, Huldbrand. I think the water punished you because I was so angry. I am so sorry—" She pulled her hand away from mine and fixed her gaze upon the window, her face dark with grief.

"Tell me what you mean," I said.

"I fear a spirit lives in the water," she said in a thin voice. "A spirit that is connected to me. I do not know exactly how. But I am afraid, Huldbrand." She looked at me, finally. "I am afraid there is a terrible truth about me."

The pain in my head grew stronger. Undine's words echoed the warning of the fisherman, the words of the priest, and even my own imaginings the night I had found her naked in the fountain. But now I fought with all my might against such superstitious thinking. "We will cover the fountain," I said. We will cover it and be safe. Then all we have left to do is to trust each other and be close. That is what you said when we spoke about the demon."

She looked at me sadly. "Yes, but I know now that you will turn against me one day, and I will not be able to bear it."

"I will never turn against you," I said.

"Yes, you will. You will forsake me, and I will be pulled into that other world. Forever."

"Stop!" I grabbed her hand.

She started to pull away from me, but I would not allow it. I held on to her as tightly as I could, as if I were holding on to my own life.

I still gripped her hand as I sank into a deep, empty sleep.

Eighteen

Once the fountain in the courtyard was covered, a creeping danger seemed to fill my estate. It slipped invisibly along the ramparts. It hovered in the moonlit courtyard late at night. It blew through the shadowy passageways of the castle. There was no name for this danger. It had no shape that I could draw, no sound I could imitate.

The servants also grew frightened. They whispered of a clammy, cold presence in the hallways. Some showed me unexplained drops of water on the stone walls, puddles in high rooms that had no leaks. My groom confided he felt something evil lurking near the stable in the dark hour before dawn. And in the courtyard itself, the air was cold and smelled of wet, dark soil.

As the days passed, Undine grew more withdrawn. When Lady Bertalda began to talk of returning home, I begged her to stay a bit longer, hoping her steady, calm presence might help Undine. And more than that— Bertalda's presence had become a great solace to me, for I was also growing more anxious and lonely each day. My reason might have taken flight entirely if Bertalda had not been there to help me.

But then one day, Bertalda herself nearly went mad. On a gray evening when I returned from one of my farms, a servant met me at the door and reported that Lady Bertalda was hiding in the anteroom of her chambers. I went to the guest quarters and found her huddled in a corner, trembling as her maids stood helplessly by.

I knelt beside her and spoke softly. "What has happened? Tell me, what?"

"I saw it," she said, her teeth chattering. "I—I saw it."

"What did you see?"

She could not answer, but hid her face with a shudder and began to weep. I ordered her servants to leave us. Then I stroked her yellow hair and spoke soothingly, begging her to tell me what she had seen.

Again, she stared at me with fearful eyes. In one quick moment she had been transformed from a strong, confident maiden into a pale, trembling girl. I squeezed her hands, trying to bring her back to her former self. "Tell me, Bertalda, what did you see? Tell me!"

"It was not human," she whispered, "not human—"

"Tell me—what was not human?"

"As I was walking through the courtyard, out of nowhere it rushed toward me. I screamed and it vanished—"

"What was it? What rushed toward you?"

"It was like death—a ghost in white—black holes for eyes—"

A terrible dread overcame me. "So now it has entered my castle walls," I said.

"Oh, you have seen it, too, Huldbrand!" She grabbed my hands.

"Yes, yes," I whispered. I pulled her to me and embraced her. I needed comfort from her as much as she needed it from me.

"He wants *me*, not her," a voice said coldly.

I looked up to see Undine in the doorway, staring at us.

"What—what do you mean?" I said.

"The demon wants me. So why are you holding *her*?"

"I was comforting—"

"Take her—I don't care! I am going to join him. So you can both be free!"

"Undine—" I let go of Bertalda and started toward her.

But she held up her hand. "Stay away from me, Huldbrand!" she said. Then she turned and ran from Bertalda's chambers.

"Undine!"

"Go after her, Huldbrand!" said Bertalda. "Please, save her!"

Before I left Bertalda, I called a guard and told him to watch over her.

Then I ran after Undine. But when I came to the

main hall, a servant told me she had left the palace. I grabbed my sword and ran outside. Shouting her name, I made a frantic search of the castle yard. When my watchman reported seeing a figure in a white gown running through the meadow below, I grabbed my horse and galloped away from my castle.

Charging toward the meadow, I saw no sign of Undine. Bats were flapping in the twilight. A black cloud hovered overhead; thunder rolled in the distance. A mighty storm was gathering.

I abandoned my horse at the edge of the cedar woods and headed down the path toward the river. The wind was bending the trees and whistling malevolently. As I came close to the water, I saw a figure lying on the bank: Undine. Her white gown spread about her, she looked like a gull with broken wings.

Her face was hidden as I ran toward her. I reached out to touch her, and suddenly the phantom's screech split the twilight—and I found myself reaching for nothing at all. Undine had evaporated into the air! I fell back in horror. Then I started scrambling through the woods, back the way I had come. I ran like a madman, slipping, crawling, clawing my way through the marsh reeds. My mind reeled with terror—was Undine herself now a demon? Had the monster taken her shape?

As I ran from the woods into the meadow, the sky broke open. A blinding rain began to fall. As a flash of lightning lit the field, I saw the figure in white again, lying near the trees.

I approached Undine's body with dread. Then I went down on my knees and touched her. She did not move; she was unconscious. Her face was scratched, her dress torn and muddied. But I felt great relief— this time it truly was her, not a ghost.

I scooped her up from the ground and tried to stand with her against the windy rain. I stumbled toward my horse, but I could not get near him. He whinnied and stamped the ground, as if a host of spirits were attacking him.

I lay Undine down, then sank beside her. Black night had fallen. The wind blew hard through the meadow as the cold rain battered us.

Then came a deep, rumbling noise. It grew louder

and louder. I held Undine tightly and waited for this new horror to reveal itself.

The noise kept coming, as if some mighty force were plowing up the meadow. But then I heard the whinny of a horse, and a man called out, "Whoa!"

A lantern was lit. A circle of rainy light revealed two white horses yoked to a large covered wagon.

"Who is there?" the driver said. His voice was deep and hoarse. In the rainy lamplight I could not see his face, as it was shrouded by his dark hood.

"Lord Huldbrand of Ringstetten," I said. "My wife is hurt! Please help us return to my castle!"

"Climb in, and I will take you there," he said.

Undine was still unconscious as I lifted her and placed her inside the wagon, under the white tent. Cotton bedding softened the hard timber planks. The tent billowed above us in the windy night, keeping out the rain.

As the wagon rolled over the meadow, I held Undine and whispered, "Wake up—please, my love, wake up."

She moaned in the darkness. I kissed her wet, cold face. "We are safe now," I whispered.

"Where—where are we?" she murmured.

"A wagon has rescued us."

"Huldbrand—" She grasped me. "It—it tried to take me. When I got to the river—it tried to pull me down—but I wanted to be with you—I fought—"

"Shhh, be still. You are with me now." I held her tightly, trying to calm her. "I will not let you go."

"I fought—I fought the water, then ran through the woods. I fell and I ran again—"

"Shhh, I have saved you," I said. "I have saved you."

"And finally proven yourself a mortal worthy of her," came a deep, chilling voice. "Now I must take you both home."

I looked up. The wagon driver was staring back at us, but still I could not see his face.

"To Ringstetten?" I said.

"No. To the sea, where I am king."

"Who are you?"

"Her father."

I yanked off the hood of his cloak, then cried out in horror as his pale eyes gleamed at me.

Kuhleborn.

Undine's scream shattered the air.

In a terrified rage, I grabbed my sword and thrust it at Kuhleborn, but he vanished—disappeared instantly like vapor.

The horses reared up, and I was thrown backward. The wagon tipped over, and Undine and I tumbled into water. The meadow had become a raging sea.

Waves crashed against one another, sending showers of foam high into the night. As water gushed down my throat, an angry current pulled me down.

But then hands gripped me and lifted me up. Undine was pulling me through the water—miraculously dragging me along a path of moonlight, away from the swirling current.

I felt my strength return, and I began to swim with her. Arm over arm, we moved beside each other, guided by the shimmering moonlight that stretched to the shore of the meadow. The wind and rain had stopped, and the sky was bright with cold stars. The storm had ceased.

Undine reached the high ground first and helped me out of the flood. We collapsed into the tall grass, and I held her tightly to me. We had saved each other from the mad spirit that had haunted us. The thought that Undine might be the daughter of a sea spirit seemed absurd as I embraced her human flesh and kissed her human lips. When we finally slept, two swans glided through my dreams, sliding toward sunrise.

Nineteen

After the night of the storm, a new peace settled over our lives. We never spoke of Kuhleborn's words. It was as if our nightmare had been thrown into the waves; Evil had been washed away, and only that which was good and true remained.

I posted guards near my river, but neither Kuhleborn nor his ghostly specter appeared there again. Our victory seemed to have vanquished our inner demons as well: I no longer looked upon Undine with suspicion and fear, and she seemed free of despair.

Though Bertalda did not know the truth of our strange story, she also seemed to have released her fears. She accepted our invitation to extend her visit, and for the next few weeks, the three of us enjoyed the simplest of pleasures: strolling the ramparts, sharing fine food under the trees at twilight, planning improvements to the garden and orchards.

Then one late-autumn morning, Bertalda suggested we go on a picnic. "I think it would be lovely to visit the Black River and sit on the bank under the trees."

I saw a flicker of fear in Undine's eyes; she had not been to the river since the night of the flood. But she quickly said, "Yes, I think I would like that, too."

"Perhaps we should go to the meadow instead," I said.

"No, Huldbrand," Undine whispered. "It is time to visit the river again."

Bertalda seemed to sense our fear. "Well, perhaps the meadow would be a better place for a picnic. Now that I think about it—"

"No," Undine interrupted. "It is time to visit the river. How else will I ever know if we are truly free?"

Bertalda stared wide-eyed at the two of us but said nothing. I ordered the servants to pack the carriage with food, and we set out for the Black River.

It was a beautiful day for a picnic. Smoke from our cedar-wood fire rose up through the red-leafed trees into the blue sky. Bertalda and I sat in a patch of sunlight at the river's edge, watching Undine swim.

Though Bertalda and I did not speak, I felt we were bound to each other by our love for Undine. We both seemed to draw strength and inspiration from her nature.

As we watched Undine glide through the gently flowing waters, someone stepped from behind a tree. Bertalda cried out with fear, then laughed. The intruder was only a boy.

But he was a boy I had never seen before. Exquisitely fair, with curling hair and pale blue eyes, he was barefoot and wore a white tunic.

"Hello!" said Bertalda.

The boy pulled a necklace of coral from the folds of his tunic. It shone crimson in the sunlight as he held it out to me. "Please, give this to your wife," he said to me. His voice sounded strangely hollow and aged. "To help her remember . . ."

"Oh, how lovely," breathed Bertalda, taking the necklace from him.

"To remember what?" I asked the boy.

Before he answered, Undine called from the river. When the boy saw her, he ran into the woods. I leaped up and rushed after him through the brush. "Wait!" I shouted. "Who are you?"

I watched him race away through the forest, then disappear behind the trees.

As I caught my breath, the woods felt more alive than ever. The air swelled with birdsong and the chirrup of crickets.

When I returned to our fire, I found Bertalda showing Undine the necklace and telling her about the mysterious boy.

Dripping wet, Undine held the coral and stared at it for a long moment. Then without a word, she thrust it back into Bertalda's hands. "Keep it for yourself, please," she said, and she moved to the shade of a tree.

I followed her and sat beside her. "The boy troubles you?" I said.

"Where did he come from?" she asked in a distant voice.

"Oh, surely he's a peasant child from nearby," I said. I spoke with false cheerfulness, for indeed I was troubled by the boy's pale eyes, his strange message.

"Where did he get the necklace?" she asked. "The sea coral."

"Perhaps his father is a sailor." I regretted my words immediately, for they linked the boy to the memory of Kuhleborn. "Or he might simply have stolen them—from the market or . . ."

She said nothing. She stared at the ground, hugging her knees, lost in thought.

Meanwhile, Bertalda had drifted down to the sunlit river. She was clasping the necklace and smiling rapturously at the water. Indeed the coral seemed to be working some sort of charm on her.

"Do you know what I would like more than anything in this world?" she called to us. "I should like to sail down the river in a boat."

Neither of us answered.

"Perhaps we can do it," she said. "Take a trip

together. Travel the river all the way to St. Martin. What do you think?"

"No, I am afraid not," I said.

"Oh, please! Before winter comes! Before the end of this beauty." She gestured to the pale gold willow fronds sweeping the edge of the water. "It would be lovely," she said. "Do you not agree?"

"No," I said. "I think—"

"Yes," Undine broke in. She spoke in a soft voice that only I could hear. "We must, Huldbrand. I must find out if the water demon still lives. . . . If it does, we must fight it again. Together."

Her words frightened me. I truly did not know if I had the courage to struggle with that mighty, inhuman power again.

"Undine," said Bertalda. "Please, can we all take a trip on the river? Soon?"

"If you wish," came Undine's faint reply.

Bertalda clapped happily. While she chatted about the sights we would see along the way, I stared at a scarlet leaf that had fallen into the water. As the gurgling current dragged it away, I felt an inexplicable grief.

 Twenty

Though lovely, clear waters splashed against the hull of our boat and birdsong fluted through the crisp, clear air, I soon regretted our journey.

Undine was distant and elusive. She kept to herself as we drifted downstream; and whenever we went ashore, she left us to explore the riverbank alone.

On the second night of our journey, we camped under a cool autumn sky. As the boatmen fed dead branches to our fire, Undine slipped away.

I sat alone with Bertalda. Silently we watched the flames crackle and leap into the black sky.

"Where do you think she has gone?" Bertalda finally asked.

"I believe she heard the river call," I said.

Bertalda sighed. "I do not know why I forced you and Undine to make this journey. I do not know what came over me. It seemed a lovely idea at the time—the water and fresh air. But ever since we have been on the river, I have had an uneasy feeling."

Just then, Undine burst upon our campsite. She was soaked to the skin. "I caught it!" she exclaimed.

"What?" I said.

"The otter. He had captured a river rat. But I grabbed him and shook him till he let it go." As she smiled at us, her eyes burned in the firelight, and she seemed more animal than human.

In that moment, I felt closer in spirit to Bertalda, with her steadiness and common sense. Perhaps if I had quickly embraced Undine—held her and loved her—we might have avoided the horror to come. But instead, I recoiled from her. I got up and went off to bed without a word.

The next morning, we drifted down the river, lost in our own worlds. Bertalda seemed drowsy as she leaned over the side of the boat and trailed her coral necklace through the water.

I sensed Undine had been wounded by my coldness, for all morning she was silent as she sat alone and stared at the flowing current.

Suddenly Bertalda screamed.

I was at her side immediately. "What happened?"

"My necklace!" she cried. "A hand reached up from the water and stole it!"

Horror crept over me, but I clung to reason. "You must have been dreaming," I said. "You must have dropped off to sleep and let go of it."

"No! No! I saw it," she whispered, clutching me frantically. "It was a hideous green hand!"

The boatmen glanced fearfully at the river. They murmured in low tones to one another. I feared they might turn against us; such simple souls believe completely in fairy magic and sorcery.

"She was dreaming, only dreaming," I said to reassure them.

"No!" cried Bertalda. "I saw the hand of a monster!"

I looked at Undine. She was hardly paying attention to Bertalda as she stared at the water. It disturbed me that she seemed so unaware of us.

"Let us return to Ringstetten," said Bertalda. "I want to go back." She hugged herself and trembled with fear.

"Yes, let us go back," I said. I turned again to Undine. She was holding her hand over the side of the boat, dipping it into the river. I saw her silently mouth words to the water. Then to my surprise, she pulled up the coral necklace. "Bertalda!" she called. "Look! I found it!"

Bertalda stared at the necklace dripping in the clammy air. "H-How?" she stammered.

"There was no monster," said Undine. She handed the coral back to Bertalda. "Only a piece of driftwood. It must have caught on a branch as it floated by. You mistook the mossy wood for a green hand."

"No, no," whispered Bertalda, "it *was* a hand." She warily placed the coral on the deck of the boat, away from her. Then she covered her face with her hands and shuddered.

I snatched up the necklace and moved quickly

to Undine. "How did you find this?" I whispered angrily. "What magic words did you say to the water?"

"What?" She looked stunned. "I said only a prayer."

"You are lying!" I whispered.

"Huldbrand—"

"What did you say? Tell me!"

She stared at me without answering. I grabbed her arm. "Do you sport with the demon?"

Her eyes narrowed in anger. "No. Let go of my arm, please," she said in a low voice.

I dropped my hand, defeated, confused. Perhaps she spoke the truth; and it was I who consorted with the underworld by entertaining such superstitious thoughts.

Undine turned away from me. She sat alone and tilted her face toward the sun and closed her eyes; closed them against me, I supposed, against my accusations and outbursts. I called to the boatmen and told them to turn the vessel around. But our retreat did not bring us relief. Instead, the air seemed more ominous than ever. A long, fat snake slithered onto a rock, licking the air. As the glaring white heat bore down upon us, the river became muddy and dense, unlike the clear waters we had sailed through only a short while ago.

Then the river began to behave in a most bizarre way. Though there was not a breath of wind and the dying yellow leaves of the willows were still, the river began to churn and ripple in jerky, unpredictable patterns. Wave after wave slapped the side of the boat, each a bit higher than the last. The river birds cawed madly, as if screaming warnings.

The boatmen whispered among themselves and glanced suspiciously at the three of us, believing, I'm sure, that we were somehow responsible for what was happening.

Bertalda also seemed frightened as she scowled at the glaring sky.

Only Undine appeared undisturbed. Her eyes closed, her lips barely parted, she seemed to be napping peacefully. My anger toward her rose like the waves lashing the side of the boat.

I shook her arm. Her eyes opened. Her expression

begged me not to be angry with her, but my heart would not soften. "How can you lie there dreaming?" I said. "Tell me what is happening to you!"

She said nothing, but gently pulled away from me.

"How can you sleep?" I demanded. "How? Do you not sense something horrible is about to happen?"

"Calm yourself," she whispered, leaning close to me. "Do not be angry with me near the water. Please."

I knew she was right. I knew the water was the home of our enemy; the demon spirit was clearly nearby. But I could not help myself. Fear and anger held me in their grip. "Where did you come from?" I said to her.

"What do you mean?"

"You were not born to the fisherman and his wife."

"What?"

"He told me. They found you as an infant. They do not know where you really came from. Who are you? Are you even human?"

She turned pale and stared at me for a long moment. Then she lay back again, closing her eyes.

I should have comforted her, but I could not control

my temper. The slithering of the snake, the unearthly stillness of the willows, the rising of the waves, the cawing of the birds—all were too threatening.

Suddenly Bertalda screamed and pointed at the river.

A human head was floating on the surface of the water! A head not unlike mine, with dead, staring eyes and seaweed tangled in its beard and hair. The boatmen cried out.

Undine bolted upright, and the head vanished.

We all gaped dumbstruck at the river as Undine lay back and closed her eyes once more.

At that moment, the head rose again—then two appeared, then three, four! They all had my face!

The boatmen shouted with terror as Bertalda screamed and screamed.

Undine leaped to her feet. Raising her arms above the water, she cried out in a strange language.

Instantly the heads vanished; the river was calm, the woods silent.

The boatmen and Bertalda stared at Undine. Slowly she dropped her arms and turned to me.

I felt cold, more cold than I had ever felt in my life. I stared at her with loathing and fear.

She held out her hand as if begging my forgiveness. But I could not forgive her.

She reached out to touch me, but I could not bear her touch. "Get away from me, witch," I said in a low voice.

She started to speak. But I stepped back. "Get away. Forever," I said.

She dropped her hand and blinked at me, her eyes clouded with grief.

"Goodbye, my love," she said. And in a blur of movement, she slipped over the side of the boat, into the water, leaving not the slightest ripple.

I felt as if my heart had been ripped from my chest.

"Undine!" I screamed.

The birds screamed also. This time not in warning, but in agony. They screamed in the forest. They screamed along the riverbank and all through the bleached sky.

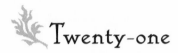 Twenty-one

I sent a grieving Bertalda home to her father. But I myself would not leave the river. I could not believe Undine was truly gone. I summoned servants from my castle, and we combed the current upstream and downstream, night and day, till finally I collapsed with fever and was carried back to Ringstetten.

Drifting in and out of sleep for days, I shivered under piles of skins and furs and kept ordering my men to dive deeper, save her, bring her back to me.

One day as an early winter storm overtook the castle, I rose and stumbled to my window. "Where is she?" I whispered madly to the falling snow, to the blackbird perched in a skeletal tree against the gray, barren sky.

Was she hiding in that tree—in the black wood and deep roots that trap life until spring? Was her fire burning underground, melting the tomb of the lord of the winter?

No. She was simply dead. She had called out to the apparition in a mysterious language born of her kinship with the wild. She had sought to protect us.

And for that crime, she now lay in some gray shadowland at the bottom of the river, her eyelids turned to ice, her lips to stone.

I pounded my wooden table, my chair, the door to my chambers. Servants rushed into the room. I shouted at them to leave me alone.

I found the castle door, pulled its bolt, and stumbled into the snow.

The wind hissed over the ground, swirling clouds of icy powder in its wake. The forsaken landscape was cold and empty but for tiny bird tracks.

Servants watched me from the kitchen. Did they think I was mad as I beat the trees and kicked the frozen ground?

I turned and shouted at those who stared, "Where is she? Where?" As I shook my fist, the pale faces at the windows vanished like ghosts, leaving me alone.

I took my horse from the stables. He snuffled in the cold air and shied away as I tried to steady myself against the wind. Finally I clutched his mane and heaved myself onto his back. "Find her," I commanded him. I held on tightly as he cracked the icy grass of the meadow with his hooves.

In the winter twilight, we trotted along the bank of the frozen Black River, past the bony, quaking arms of the bare trees.

"Undine!" I cried against the wind. "Undine!"

There was no answer.

"Undine!"

This last cry unbalanced me; I flew from my mount into a deep snowbank, then started crawling toward the river.

I clawed at the thick blanket of snow that covered the frozen water. "Give her back to me!" I cried. I beat the ice until my hands were bloody and snow covered me. I wished I were a white bear, for then I could find her . . . a white hare, I could find her . . . a white owl, I could find her. But I was only a mortal man, and I knew now for certain I would never find her—never again.

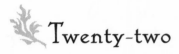 Twenty-two

When I gave up hope of rescuing Undine from the frozen river, I gave up hope of ever again feeling exhilaration or passion. I shut myself in my castle for the rest of the winter and felt my heart turn to ice.

Spring crept slowly upon Ringstetten: first came the buds on the trees, then a pair of geese on the river, followed by a downy gosling.

Soon white violets began to appear among the ash-gray grasses of winter; a tree frog piped at dusk; a fresh anthill grew on the road. And what was once malevolent and unyielding began gently to open its fist. Branches spread full into leaf, and once-barren trees gave birth to birds who sang all morning.

On one such sun-filled day, Bertalda returned.

Her carriage arrived unexpectedly, and when she stepped out of it, resplendent in a lavender gown, she was a soothing vision.

"Huldbrand," she greeted me kindly, "I have come to help you prepare your castle for the spring."

We embraced each other silently and mournfully, for we shared the unspoken burden of Undine's death. Bertalda blamed herself for forcing us to take the river journey, and I, of course, blamed myself for my loss of temper and courage.

But Bertalda did not let our burdens weary her. With her typical industriousness, she set about revitalizing Ringstetten. At first I followed dumbly in her wake as grateful as the servants for her restoration of order.

She began by updating my accounts and consulting with the chief cook and chamberlain. She urged me to practice tilting with my squires, to oversee the cutting of the forest, to visit the fields flooded with spring rain, and to plan for the sowing of oats, beans, and barley.

In the weeks that followed, we lived as sister and

brother, as kind companions to each other. One day we supervised the shearing of my lambs. The next day we rose before dawn and traveled to the nearest city market. We met with the town's sheriff and with wool sellers, and after our prices were agreed upon, we headed happily home.

On other days, we avoided work and entertained ourselves by galloping through the woods, hawking and hunting. We attended tournaments at nearby estates.

At night, Bertalda gave me lessons on the harp or taught me words of Latin, or we played chess with her chessmen—dragons and giants made of carved whalebone. Before bedtime, we toured my palace together, locking the doors and making certain all was well. Then we gently touched hands and retired to our separate chambers.

Our time together was without passion. But it was quite comforting, and slowly it helped free me from the terrible grief of losing Undine. I forced myself to forget her soft laughter, her pale blue eyes, and her wild, innocent ways. I said goodbye to her each time I sent a falcon into the air, each time Bertalda and I locked the palace doors against the dark night.

Then one day, a new grief presented itself. As Bertalda and I sat together in the garden—she stitching a sun into her needlework and I sketching a design for the replanting of young pear trees—the gong sounded at the gate. To our astonishment, the duke had arrived.

Once he was given food and drink, Bertalda took her leave of us. Though unspoken, it was clear there was a dire purpose to his visit, and he wished to speak with me alone.

I invited him to my hall and offered him the best tobacco and a silver cup of wine. Settled comfortably before the fire, the dignified gentleman cleared his throat and said, "I am her father, you know. I must protect her honor."

"I understand," I said. It was a simple task to trace the rest of his thought. Lady Bertalda could not continue to live in my castle alone with me. It was not proper.

"She must return to St. Martin," he said.

I nodded.

But later I could not sleep. I awoke at midnight, cold with sweat, my heart pounding. I cannot lose Bertalda, too, I thought. I will drown in my loneliness if I lose her.

I rose from my bed and paced like a trapped animal about my room. There was only one answer. *I must marry her*, I told myself.

I could not wait for dawn; I feared that Bertalda might slip away before then, like water between my fingers, like Undine over the side of the boat.

As I stalked the dark passageways of my palace toward her chambers, I heard the plaintive sound of a maid singing the Psalms. There was a chill in the air; a wind seemed to blow right through me. As my fear drove me toward Bertalda, I became lost. In my own castle, I could not find her chambers. I felt my way along the cold, damp stone. "Bertalda!" I cried.

A door opened—the flicker of a candle, the rustle of a nightdress, the sound of feet upon the stone floor— and she was there beside me.

"What is it?" she said.

In the twinkling candlelight, I touched her soft gown. "Please, do not leave me," I said. "Stay and marry me."

"Yes, I will, of course," she whispered. She put down her taper and took my face in her smooth hands and kissed me.

As we embraced, I heard the maid singing her hymn, and I heard a strange rushing sound—as if a giant wave had just crashed upon some distant, dark shore.

Twenty-three

The duke gave us his blessing, then set off for home to share the news with his family. I sent a messenger to summon the priest from the abbey at St. Martin.

Meanwhile, Bertalda and I began preparing for our celebration. We decided to have our wedding at Ringstetten. Guests were invited from far and wide, and clothing and furs were ordered from St. Martin for Bertalda's trousseau.

On the day her trunks arrived, servants spread the bright garments over the grass so they might air in the sunlight. A cheerful array of red taffeta, purple silk, black sable, and white ermine dotted our lawn as Bertalda and I sat under the canopy of a shade tree and went over the cook's list of banquet dishes.

We were interrupted by the sound of the gong ringing on the turret. Then a servant rushed toward us. "My lord, the priest from the monastery of St. Martin has arrived."

I was surprised to see the bearded holy man stride toward us with a look of unhappy determination on his face. Why did he not return my welcoming smile as I rose to greet him?

The mystery deepened when he would not take the hand I offered but clung instead to his beads. "Lord Huldbrand," he said, "I am afraid I do not bring you good tidings."

I asked him to step inside so we might speak alone. But he waved his hand. "There is no need for us to be alone," he said. "What I have to say concerns Lady Bertalda as well. So please, allow me to speak now."

I nodded.

"Are you absolutely certain Undine is dead?"

Bertalda gasped. I could only stare at the priest.

"I believe she is not," he said in a fierce whisper.

"But why?" I asked.

"These past few days she has come to me in

dreams. Wringing her hands in anguish, she says, 'I am alive, Holy Father. I swear it: I am still alive.'"

A chill went through me. Bertalda cried out. I slipped my arm around her and held her close to me. "But those are only dreams," I said to the priest. "You have no proof that she lives. Do you?"

He shook his head. "No, yet I am convinced you should not marry another, Lord Huldbrand," he said.

"I am sorry, but I think neither of us could tolerate separating from the other," I said. "Will you not marry us?"

"I shall not," he said. He turned to Bertalda. "Part from him, my lady. Can you not see he turns pale even upon hearing the name of his beloved?"

Bertalda moaned as if she might faint. I grabbed her, then turned on the priest. "Do not frighten her! You poisoned me before with your superstitions! Are you trying to drive me mad?"

As I helped Bertalda to our bench, the priest shook his head.

"Go, please!" I ordered him. "I'll send for a priest who is not in the thrall of ignorance and superstition."

The priest left. But his gloomy pronouncements cast a pall on our preparations. The situation worsened when a seafarer brought word from the fisherman. It seemed his mad wife had also been having strange dreams, and she, too, was fearful of my impending marriage.

I did not share this troubling news with Bertalda. And I myself shook off the eerie warnings by asserting as I had before, that neither the priest nor the fisherfolk should be taken seriously. When a monk from a nearby cloister cheerfully consented to marry us, I dropped whatever lingering doubts I had. Indeed, over the last few months, all my fears and passions seemed to have succumbed to the dissecting hands of reason, leaving me bereft of great feeling for anything.

To further flaunt superstition, I decided the castle fountain should flow for our wedding, so I ordered servants to roll away the great boulder that covered its source.

At first, as I stood with my workmen in the courtyard, I feared that the spring had dried up again, for only a trickle of water came forth. But slowly the flow grew stronger until a sparkling shower burst high into the spring air.

During the next few days, long tables were set up in the garden, and a tent of purple silk was raised. The palace floors were swept and covered with fresh herbs and roses. Tapestries and pieces of silk were hung on the walls. Hogs were roasted over fires, and geese were slaughtered by the butcher. Three swans were even killed and prepared for the event: the night before the ceremony, their beaks were painted gold and their bodies silver, and they were set upon beds of pastry.

On the day of our wedding, Bertalda was in her chambers, dressing for the marriage procession. As young girls entwined golden ribbons in her long braids, the housemaids decked our bridal bed with fresh linens.

Down in the stables, I visited the tall white horses waiting for us. Both were outfitted with gold harnesses.

The grooms reported to me that villagers were already lining the road, ready to give us silver coins for luck as we paraded from the castle to the church. Flute players and harpists were in the outer ward, preparing to lead the procession.

Soon it was time for me to dress in my finest cape and strap on my jeweled sword. I left the stables and proceeded back to the palace.

As I strode through the courtyard, a cloud passed over the sun, and all at once the hour seemed more like dusk than morning. I was cheered, though, when I heard Bertalda's laughter ring from an upstairs window.

But then a wind gusted through the courtyard, spraying droplets of fountain water over me. The flow of the fountain grew stronger, and an arc of water seemed to climb the air toward Bertalda's window.

I was afraid for her. But then the waters grew calm.

I relaxed, too. There—I had slipped again into an old way of thinking, I told myself—I had imagined personality and motive where there was none. It was only a fountain; it was only water.

The wind gusted again; the surrounding trees clattered in the gray air. Nothing to fear, I thought quickly; perhaps we were about to experience a sudden storm. I worried that Bertalda would be disappointed if we could not travel in our splendid procession.

She, however, seemed unaware of the change in the weather, for again her laughter rang from the upstairs window.

The fountain waters suddenly exploded into the air and arched over me. Then they crashed down upon the courtyard. The waters burst again and again into the sky in great columns. They showered down upon the courtyard in spangled, rainbow-colored arcs. The waters were going mad.

There was no way I could escape. I tried to flee, but a thick white fog now blanketed the ground. My palace had vanished in the mist. I heard Bertalda's laughter no more.

I was lost. Turning back to the fountain, I cried out for help. The raging cascade subsided, and the waters began whirling into a funnel. I watched, transfixed, as they swirled into the shape of a woman: a woman veiled in a white shroud, like the demon-ghost. Slowly she began moving toward me.

Twenty-four

I stared with horror as the white figure emerged from the fountain. As she glided toward me, her feet did not touch the ground.

"Huldbrand," she said in a hollow, distant voice.

"Undine," I breathed. I was frozen to the spot as she drew closer and closer.

I imagined the demon's face beneath her veil: no eyes, no lips—only black holes in a white death's head.

I wanted to flee, but her voice stopped me. "Alas," she said, "will you not look upon me again?"

I could not breathe as she raised her hands and uncovered her face. I stared into her pale blue eyes as they glistened with tears. Tears spilled down her rose-colored cheeks, and I saw that she was even more beautiful than I had remembered.

Without a word, she wrapped her arms around me and kissed my lips. Then I kissed her wet eyelids and her soft cheeks. As I breathed in her sweet scent, unspeakable joy and sorrow washed over me. I remembered our days together.

"Where were you?" I whispered mournfully. "Why have you waited so long to come back to me?"

She did not answer. As I pressed my face against her hair, I pleaded, "Tell me—where have you been? Why did you not come back till now?"

Still she did not answer. She only wept.

"Tell me!" I was weeping now also. I started to pull back from her so I might look again at her face, but she held me so tightly I could not move.

We embraced a moment more; then I started to pull away again. But again she would not release me.

She pressed herself against me and wept. She wept as if she would weep away her heart. Her tears fell like rain. I could not stand under their weight.

My strength was gone. I started to sink to the stone courtyard, for I could not breathe. She was weeping me to death.

Then I heard singing—strange, beautiful singing. The wings of a great swan brushed against me. As the heavy wings fanned my flesh, I was blinded by the thick, swirling fog. Then the swan lifted me from the ground and began to carry me away.

The swan was singing as we flew through the billowing clouds beyond my castle of Ringstetten, beyond the Black River, beyond the duke's kingdom and the fisherman's woods, beyond the marks of the compass and the Sea of Darkness.

The singing did not cease as we soared above a lonely shore. Gulls accompanied us as we glided down over the foam-crested sea. We skimmed the surface of the water. Then my avian mount plunged me down into the waves, down into the cold abyss, down into the maw of the primeval ocean.

All the while the swan was singing, and I knew that I was dead.

How best to describe our life now?

We rise together each dawn and float through a stream of shadow and light. Stilt-legged creatures and sprays of tiny fish move about the waving sea grass and crimson coral of our garden.

We drift with the drag and pull of the waves. We climb the pale, luminous waters to more shallow seas, then fly with the racing current, leap through foaming breakers, and swim with whales and dolphins.

When the tides change, and moonlight shimmers over the top of our world, we return to the deep-sea palace of the sea king. And there, in the black silence of the night, Undine and I pour into each other.

And so our life together flows on, through an eternity of water.

MARY POPE OSBORNE is the author of many books, including the Magic Tree House series, which has sold more than thirty million copies and been published in more than twenty countries around the world. She came across the German fairy tale "Undine" as she was researching her book *Mermaid Tales from Around the World.* She says, "I decided it deserved a book all its own. My novel has departed considerably from the original, but I gratefully acknowledge the inspiration of this classic tale."